BLACK-HEARTED

By: Kyeate

STAY CONNECTED

Facebook: Kyeate TheAuthor or Kyeate Holt

Reading Facebook Group: Kyewritez & Thingz

Instagram: Kyewritez

WHEN SHIT GOT REAL...

The dark skies and humid temperature had me in a trance. Sitting on the hood of the car, I blew the weed smoke from my mouth and stared off into the darkness. The many voices could be heard around me, but I had tuned everyone out. Today had been the worst day of my life. Watching someone that you love dearly being placed in the dirt can put a different type of pain in your heart. My life was already fucked up as is, but now I had nothing else to live for, and I gave zero fucks of the outcome.

"Don, you heard what I said bruh?" my homie Loc spoke, breaking me from my trance. Looking at him, I took another pull of the blunt.

Silence.

"You sure you good? I know when you zone out like this you on some other shit. Moms calling, so I got to head to the crib see that she straight and shit," Loc said.

Loc was my best friend. If you see me, you saw him, and it was no other way around.

"I'm good," I mumbled. That's what my mouth said, but my head was already gone and ready to act on what I had planned out.

"Cool, I'll be back around here later on," Loc said and dapped me up.

As Loc walked off in the distance, I glanced back at the porch where my mother and her friends sat somberly drinking their sorrows away. I could never take this pain from her, but what I had to do was for Donna.

At fifteen years old, I was the man of the house, and that was something that I took pride in. It was nobody but my sister, our mother, and me.

Flicking the remainder of the blunt in the street, I looked back at the porch, giving my mama one last look before heading off down the road. Walking the two blocks to my destination, I had been peeping the scene ever since his name popped up. Supposedly he had left town, but that's just what they wanted us to think. As I stood in front of his house, the home was dark as if nobody was home. Looking over my shoulders and around me, once the coast was clear, I continued to the back of the house.

Quietly walking on the gravel, the smell of weed hit my nose. When I rounded the corner, I don't know if this was a setup or not, but there was no way that God was letting this come to me this easy. There he was standing on the back porch like a dumb ass as if nothing were wrong.

Walking forward, the crunching of the gravel caused him to look my way.

"The fuck is that?" he asked. I walked closer so that he could make out my face.

"Aw, damn, Don, you can't be creeping up on a nigga like that." He laughed and blew out the smoke.

"Sorry I ain't get to make it to your sister's funeral today. I just got back in town," he lied.

"Man, fuck you! You ain't show your face because you know what the fuck you did to my sister. You were the one person she trusted, but as soon as she tells your ass no, you decide to rape her and leave her for dead on the side of the road, my nigga!" I spat.

The way his face changed was guilt within itself because I know he wanted to know how the fuck I knew this shit.

"Yeah, I've been knowing it was you this whole time. You ran your mouth to the wrong people!" I spat.

"Little nigga, and so what you gone do? Ain't you like twelve?"

This nigga had the nerve to laugh. I started laughing right along with him. Removing the gun from my waistband, he shut the fuck up just as quickly.

"Bitch, I'm fifteen, and you about to die," I said, lifting the gun and letting off seven shots.

The smoke from the gun filled the air as I watched him hit the ground. The blood flowing from him had me close my eyes, remembering the bruises on my sister's body.

The porch light came on, and somebody came running outside. The screams of his mother were the same ones that my mother cried. The sound was satisfying to my ears.

Slowly, I turned on my heels and walked out of the backyard and back down the street. I just wanted to tell my mother the truth.

By the time I made it home and up on the porch with my mother and her friends, the sirens could be heard in the background.

"Where you been, Don?" She looked up and saw the gun in my hand.

"I killed that nigga that raped Donna. The police are coming. I just want you to know that I love you, but it had to be done. It might not bring Donna back, but he won't hurt nobody else."

I looked at her, and her eyes began to water.

"I already lost one child, why would you do this, Don?" she cried.

"Son, I need for you to drop the gun," the officer said, walking into the yard.

I sat the gun down and placed my hands on my head. Slowly I walked backwards to the officer with my eyes still on my mama's tear-stained face. Inside, I felt so liberated for taking that nigga's life, and I would do it all over again for my sister.

CHAPTER 1

DONMIR "DON" TELHIDE

Twelve Years Later

S trolling through the yard, I watched as motherfuckers moved out the way like I was parting the Red Sea. A few head nods here and there and even a few mugs, but these niggas knew what was up. My release day was coming up, and niggas hated that shit. They would do anything in they power to keep a nigga from getting released, but they knew not to cross me.

I've been in the cage for twelve years after killing that bitch ass nigga that hurt my sister, and this was the life I had gotten accustomed to. I spent two years in juvie before they sent me up the road to an adult prison. Now, at twenty-seven, it was time for me to enter the free world and do this shit called life.

When I got to my table, I took a seat on top, and my goons stood around. When I came on the yard, I loved my peace, and you wouldn't see me chopping it up with anybody unless they were a part of my crew.

Placing my hands underneath my chin, I looked out into the yard. My time in prison went smoothly once this OG cat name Murk took me under his wing. He was like a father figure, and he schooled me on everything. My best friend Loc was doing big things back in the city, and he been holding me down this entire bid, on top of putting me on with his plug so that I could have weight in here. I was the only one running drugs in here, and if somebody else tried, they had to see me. I had the entire prison on lock. Even the warden bought from me to support his habit.

"Aye yo, Don, can I talk to you for a minute?" I heard a voice walking up, and he didn't even make it to the table before my crew stopped him.

"Can't you see a nigga's enjoying his peaceful time. The fuck you want nigga?" I spat.

"Um, um, I was trying to see if I could get something off you?"

"Ion know what you talking about, and you need to back the fuck away from this table because obviously, you don't know shit about me to walk up to me and ask me some bullshit like that. If you value your life, you better turn around and don't step to me again," I stated calmly.

Everyone in this bitch knew not to approach me the way this nigga did, and for them to allow this nigga to walk to my table, they must want him dead.

"Aye!" I called out, and he slowly turned around. When I looked at the young dude, something in him pulled at that one damn heart string I had.

"Let him through," I demanded. My homies looked at me like I was crazy but knew not to question me. They moved out the way and let him through.

I pointed to the bench in front of me, signaling for him to take a seat. I could tell everyone was shocked because all eyes were on us.

"Who the fuck sent you over here to me?" I asked. Due to his fidgeting, I knew he was nervous.

"Don't make me ask you again."

"Toolie told me that if I could get something off you that he would erase my debt. I owed that nigga when we were out in the streets, and I ain't got shit in here to pay him with. That nigga's foul, and I know he's probably on some bullshit." He sighed.

"What you in here for?" I asked.

"Killing my mom's old man. The nigga couldn't keep his hands to himself." He sighed.

I nodded my head because I knew exactly what he meant. I would do that shit all over again for my sister.

"Toolie knows better, and he tried to set you up. Don't worry about him, and don't run with nobody in here. They will keep you safe. Y'all hear me, even when I'm gone watch over him," I told the others.

"I appreciate that, man. I ain't no hoe ass nigga, but I just want to do my time in peace. All I asked him was to give me time to get on my feet in here, then I got him, but that nigga wasn't try- ing to hear shit," he said.

All I did was nod my head. No words were needed.

"Take your place," I told him, signaling for him to get his ass up from the table.

When I looked out into the yard, I locked eyes with Too- lie and hit him with a smirk. I don't know what that nigga had against me, but he just wanted to keep stirring up problems.

Throughout my time here, I took the time to find myself. Let me quit fucking lying. I found part of me, but I didn't give a fuck about much. Every time I closed my eyes, I saw my sister in that casket, and no matter what, and no matter how long it has been, that shit was fresh as hell with me.

I had a few hours left in this bitch, and at midnight I was gone. The taste of freedom was anxious and almost like a home cook meal that was waiting on me. It was highly anticipated.

Once I had gotten enough sun, I stood up from the table and stretched. Popping my knuckles, I moved through the crowd, making sure I made my way over to Toolie. Toolie started to make his way toward me as I walked over to him.

"Lil homie's debt is cleared, and not one hair on his head is to be touched!" I spat and bumped his little ass out the way.

Once back inside, I headed to my cell and waited on collections and my right-hand.

Over the years, the man in me formed. Being under Murk, he was a soulless nigga, so I couldn't help to pick up off him. He always told me in order for my time to go by fast that I needed to only focus on the shit I could see, and not the outside world. So, besides talking to Loc and running this business, I didn't know shit about anything going on outside of these walls. Pussy was handed to me in here because the officers were the biggest freaks. All I needed was some top, and I was good. These hoes see and know a nigga getting money in here and see it as a meal ticket. They really be trying to get pregnant by a nigga.

Looking up, I saw my right hand walked in the cell.

"Here is everything that has been transferred to a card for you. The warden said he would have it ready when you leave tonight. You need anything else?" he asked.

"Nah, just make sure you keep running shit the same. If you need anything, you know you can call me. Toolie might try some shit when I leave, but don't let that nigga slide. There is still no product to be coming in here but mine. I don't mind coming back up in here after hours and shake shit up if you can handle it," I told him.

"Shit, you know I got this shit under control. The question is, are you ready for the outside world? It's been twelve long years, my nigga. You know shit ain't the same from when you were fifteen," he told me.

"I know enough to get by out there. I'm just focusing on this money and shit. That's it," I replied.

We shook it up, and I stood to give him a brotherly hug because I knew this was the last time that I would see him.

"Stay up, Don, I love you fool."

"Love don't love nobody," I replied like I did when everybody mentioned that shit. All he did was laugh, and he left my cell.

CHAPTER 2

DON

W hen I walked out of the bathroom from changing, I looked down at my clothing and already felt like a million bucks. Loc had got me right for release. A nigga needed to see a barber before anything, but at this point, I didn't give a shit and was ready to go.

When I stepped out of the room, the warden was standing there waiting.

"Anything you need, you know I got you. You left orders for everything, right?" he asked. I nodded my head.

"You may go," he told me.

Grabbing the few things that I brought with me, I headed to the exit. I ain't gone lie. A nigga's nerves were all over the place because I was about to be a free man. I did that twelve years like a G.

As soon as the door opened, I looked up and saw my dog Loc standing there on a fresh ass Audi.

"My nigga!" he called out, and I walked toward him.

We both dapped each other and pulled each other in for a brotherly hug.

"Man, homie, I've been waiting on this shit forever. A nigga miss you out here. I can't enjoy all this wealth without my bro." He sighed.

"You done got soft on me, my nigga?" I joked. He knew I was shooting the shit, so all he did was laugh.

"Man, fuck all that. Let's get the fuck out of here and to your new home. As soon as you get your license, this motherfucker here is yours," he told me as I looked at the black on black Audi with the chrome feet.

"Damn, I guess I missed out on all the basic shit, huh?" I asked and slid in the passenger seat. As soon as my body hit the leather, Loc handed me a freshly wrapped blunt and a cup of Hennessey.

"Good looking," I nodded and took a toke of the blunt. Loc started the car and turned the music up as I let the smoke take over my mind and vibed to the music.

"When you get settled, Win wants to have a meeting with you. That nigga is impressed with how you were running the inside, and he wants to see that shit on the streets as well," Loc informed me.

"I still run that shit inside even while I'm out here. Ain't nothing running through them walls but my shit, and the warden fucks with me, so he's still gone get that cash as well."

"How you feeling, though, bro on some real shit? You a grown ass man now, and things are different. Do you regret anything?" Loc had the nerve to ask me.

I slowly turned my head and blew the smoke out.

"You deadass asking me that? I don't regret shit and I'll do that shit a million times for my sister. Nobody saw the shit that my moms and I had to see, and almost every time I close my eyes, I see my sister's body. I wish a motherfucker would approach me for murking that nigga. I feel like any person would after avenging someone they love death. Had that been you, I would've done the same shit, and you know it!" I snapped and took a swig of the dark liquor.

"Chill the fuck out. I'm not the one to be snapping on. You know that I know how you feel, but that's why I'm asking. That shit put you in a dark place mentally, and I know sometimes that shit will fuck with you. You will need all your focus working with Win because he doesn't like personal shit getting in the way with making his money," Loc spoke as he slowed down and turned into some condos.

"I made that nigga enough money with no problems, so I can handle that shit." I shrugged.

"These streets different, though, but here these are yours," he said, handing me a pair of keys. Them the keys to your whip and your place. Come on. I got some shit set up for you." He smirked.

"I hope you ain't got no bitch up in here where I plan to lay my damn head. You know I don't trust that shit." I looked at him.

"Nigga, if you don't take your ass in the house. I'm going to pick up shorty around the corner. I'm gone have her ass blind-folded. Stop fading me like I don't know your dark ass." He laughed.

"Yeah, aite, what's the addy?" I asked.

"It's 3B, right there where ole girl is walking up the steps. Well, stumbling, she looks off her ass," Loc said, and I turned my attention to the shorty that was walking but stopped.

"Aite, hurry back," I told him and hopped out the car.

Walking up the steps, the girl was all giggling and mumbling to herself, and I ain't want no parts since she was talking to herself. That was until when I got to the step behind her, and she couldn't keep her balance. If I weren't there to catch her, she would've busted her damn ass.

"Damn shorty, you good?"

She turned around, and she had the prettiest set of eyes. Them bitches were light gray, but she was dark as cocoa. Maybe because it was dark outside, but they stood out even more as if the moonlight were shining on them bitches, but something about them made me bit my lip.

"Get your motherfucking hands off me, nigga! I don't know you!" she snapped.

"Bitch, I was just trying to keep your drunk ass from falling down the damn steps. You want some assistance because I will gladly knock your ass out and send you backwards. Out here smelling like the goddamn liquor store. Drunk ass bitch!" I barked and moved around her.

"Who the fuck you calling a bitch!" she yelled and tried to walk up on me but stumbled and tripped missing the step.

"That's what your drunk ass gets. You walking up on the wrong one." I laughed. Loc stood at the bottom of the steps.

"You good, nigga? What the fuck going on?" he asked.

"This drunk ass bitch talking out the side of her neck. I should've let that ass fall down the steps."

"Fuck you," she mumbled as she got up and ran on up the steps, I guess to her house.

"Bitch, you couldn't get this dick if I smacked your ass in the face with it." I smirked. Looking back at Loc, he was hunched over laughing.

"Why the fuck you still here, I'm ready to fuck something?" I told Loc.

"Hell, I thought you were about to put your mac down on shorty, so I was waiting, but I guess I'll head to pick up shorty." He laughed and headed back to the car.

I walked on up the steps and headed to my new crib, sliding the key in the lock. I don't know where her little crazy ass went, but I better not see her ass again.

Once I stepped inside my crib, I stood there in the middle

of the living room floor and just took everything in. After twelve years, I had my own home and didn't have to share a small ass cell with somebody. Loc had the place decked out in my favorite colors — royal blue, gray, and black.

I tossed the keys on the table and continued to walk through the place, taking it all in. My nigga had done me good. When I got to the bedroom, the king-size bed looked comfortable as hell. I slowly removed the clothing that I had on and laid it in the chair. Walking into the connecting bathroom, I turned the shower on and stepped inside.

I had to get this jail funk off of me, and I knew that shit would be embedded in my skin no matter how much I scrubbed. My mother didn't know that I was home, and she was the first person I was going to see in the morning. I wanted to surprise her.

"You gone do right, baby brother?" I heard the voice that talked to me over the years.

"I don't have no choice. I plan on it." I sighed.

"You can't hold on to this hurt forever, Don. I'm fine and at peace," she replied.

"Yeah, aite, I hear you." I nodded and turned the water off.

Stepping out the shower, I wrapped the towel around my waist and headed to the mirror. The steam had the glass fogged up, and I used another towel to wipe it clean. Looking at myself, I never told anyone that my sister always visited me. She was like the sense that I didn't have and tried to keep me on my toes. Maybe it was my subconscious, or perhaps it was her ghost. Whatever it was, I invited it because it was all I had. That's why every time I closed my eyes, I saw her because I have never let her go.

I heard voices coming from the living room. Turning toward the hallway, I saw Loc walking down.

"Nigga you kept a key for yourself?"

"I knocked on the door, but it's only for emergencies. You

got a key and the code to my spot as well. But look, I'm finna head over to this shorty that I talk to that say a few buildings over. As soon as you're done here, hit me, and I'll come back and get her. You like?" he asked as I walked into the living room and saw this thick ass redbone standing there in a trench coat, eyes covered.

Her body was cool, but I wasn't worried about shit else but getting my dick wet and sending her on her way.

"She cool," I told him.

As soon as Loc left out the door, I took a seat on the couch and opted on if I wanted her to take the blindfold off. I really didn't even want her to look at me. I could tell from her pouty lips that she had a nice mouth on her.

"Turn toward my voice, but don't take the blindfold off," I demanded. She slowly turned toward me, and I stood up in front of her.

"Open your mouth?" I demanded. When she opened her mouth, I took in her breath, and she had the prettiest set of teeth.

"Smile," I ordered. With no hesitation, she did as she was told.

"Can I take this blindfold off? Damn, you sound good as hell," she spoke.

I placed my finger to her lips. "Sssh, only talk when spoken to," I answered.

Using my hand, I removed her coat, letting it hit the floor. My eyes roamed her entire body, and I was thoroughly pleased with what I saw. My dick rocked up, and I grabbed her hand, placing it on my shit.

"You can handle all this?" I asked, and I watched as she nodded her head and bit down on her lip. I took a seat back on the couch and guided her in between my legs.

"Suck this shit, then!" I spat. I knew my first nut would be fast, so I wanted her to suck that shit out.

As I leaned my head on the back of my couch, shorty went to work and did her thing. That blindfold wasn't stopping her at all. She knew her way around the dick. I wasn't one to make noise, but she almost got a tenor out of me. She did some shit with my balls, and I felt my shit rising to the tip. It was like she knew exactly what to do without me asking.

She pushed me further into her mouth, and I knew I had to be touching her damn tonsils, but shit, I ain't even know if the bitch had any the rate she was going. I gave that hoe a baby shower, shooting all my kids down her throat.

I had no issues with getting back up because now I was anticipating her pussy, hoping it was just as good as her head game.

Lifting her, I snatched the thin string of panties she had on off and pushed her over on the couch so that her ass was tooted up just like I needed it to be. Turning around, I saw a Magnum on the table and grabbed that shit, sliding it on my dick. When I slid in gal's shit, I was somewhat disappointed. Damn, maybe that's why her head game crucial because her pussy was wack, and the hoe ain't have no walls.

Pulling my dick out, I spat on it and slid back in, but the shit was still dry. Blowing out in frustration, I tried again only to get two good thrusts in before the shit just wasn't appeasing, and my dick went soft.

"What's wrong?" she asked, looking over her shoulder at me, still blindfolded.

"Did I ask you to speak?" I snapped. I removed the condom off my dick and bent over to pick up shorty's coat, tossing to her.

"Put that shit back on. I'm bout to call your ride!" I snapped.

"Was it not good?" she had the nerve to ask.

"You don't like to follow directions, do you? What's wrong

is your shit dry, and I almost fell in,"

"Please, I need this money." She started to cry, and I wasn't trying to hear this shit. Loc had me about to cuss his ass out.

"Yo nigga you finished already?" he spoke into the phone.

"Man, if you don't come get Sahara's no wall having ass. The fuck you get her from?" I snapped, looking back at shorty.

"I thought shorty told me her name was Keshia," he mumbled.

"I don't give a fuck what she said. The bitch pussy dry, and I couldn't move in that shit. You got five minutes or shorty's ass gone be on the steps!" I barked and hung the phone up. A nigga was pissed because I wanted some damn pussy.

"Come on, shorty. Loc's gone pay you for your troubles. Maybe you need to change professions because I don't see how you making any money off that pussy. Now your head game's the truth." I motioned her to the door and helped her on the porch.

As soon as I saw Loc pulling up, I slammed the door so hard it probably woke up the neighbors. Got me out here fucking these bum ass hoes and shit. After locking up, I headed back to the bathroom to wash my dick off and climbed in bed. This bed felt like I was lying on the clouds. My eyes got heavy and sleep took over.

CHAPTER 3

SHERITY TYREE

As soon as I made it inside and closed the door, I slid down to the floor and got myself together. I was drunk as hell, and I rarely get this drunk on a work night, but after the day I had, I needed an extra drink, not to mention that asshole I just had to cuss the fuck out. After a few moments, I got myself together and slowly peeled myself from the floor. Walking into the kitchen, I pulled me a pickle juice shot and toss it back.

When I got to my room, I removed my clothes and tossed them on the floor. My head was spinning, and I know I needed a shower, but I also knew that I couldn't stand on my feet too long. I fell onto the bed and said a mini prayer.

During my twenty-six years of life, I couldn't help but think how much of a mess it really was. I lived a double life, but it wasn't healthy. When my family disowned me, it hurt like hell, but it also gave me that push that I needed to move forward and not let that stop me from getting where I needed to go. I enrolled in college even though once I entered college, that was the start of the double life for me.

By day I was a social worker, and I took my job seriously. It was something close to my heart. Once my day was completed, I turned into a whole other being, and I numbed every ounce of me with alcohol. I had no lie to tell. I was a functional alcoholic. It was the only way I could get through this shit called life.

Relationships were nonexistent once my secret was out because no man wanted to deal with an alcoholic bitch all the time. Besides losing myself in drinking, not that it matters, but I was a healthy person. I watched what I ate and worked out faithfully. I guess it helped me mentally thinking I was balancing it all out. Slowly I closed my eyes while my drunken high took over.

◻ ◻ ◻ ◻

Stepping out the shower, I felt like a whole new woman. Last night was just a mere memory, and it was a new day. Staring back at my reflection in the mirror, I gave myself a half smile. Over the years, it took time for me to find beauty in myself again. I wanted to be so ugly because I didn't like the attention from males. After a few therapy sessions, I started to embrace my cocoa skin and my funny eyes. I used to want to keep my body covered and hide because I knew it was bomb as hell, and it was out of my control, but the attention was overwhelming.

Standing at 5'3 and weighing 145 pounds, I was perfect with my flat abs and round ass. My perfect B cup breasts set up to the point I didn't have to wear a bra. After completing my hygiene and dressing in my work out clothes, I headed to the kitchen to grab me a green juice.

It was going on seven a.m., and I always liked to go to the gym before the crowd came through there. Locking my door, I walked to the on-site gym.

Placing my AirPods in my ears, I entered the double doors and went to the treadmill. As the sounds of Meg The Stallion blasted in my ears, I started my morning cardio. I set the pace on the treadmill at a slow walking speed for about three minutes before increasing. When the sauna door opened, it startled me because I thought I was the only one in here. With his back facing me, the sweat that dripped from his body and strong back was almost mesmerizing.

He used a towel he had to wipe his neck off before pulling

a wife beater over his head. When he turned around, we locked eyes. It was like my voice was caught in my throat. I took him in from head to toe. We were the same cocoa complexion, and he was tall as hell. I could see his lips moving but heard nothing due to the music blaring in my ears. The way the wife beater hugged his chest let me know that he worked out faithfully. The grimace that graced his face had me confused. I hit pause on my phone and removed my AirPods.

"Excuse me?" I asked. I assumed he was talking to me since I was the only one in here.

"Ain't nobody said shit to you with yo drunk ass!" he snapped. Instantly my mind went back to last night and the guy that I had words with.

"Oh, it's your ass." I sighed and rolled my eyes in irritation.

He slowly made his way over to me, and I was prepared to pull my mace out if I had to. When he got close to me, he sniffed me.

"You smell better." He laughed.

He had me so fucked up in the head that I missed my step and slid off the damn treadmill falling onto the floor. Embarrassed as hell, I hopped up quick as hell.

"Aye, either you clumsy as hell or you still on that oil from last night." He held his hand out to help me up, and I smacked it away.

"I've smacked motherfuckers for less. Get yo ass up!" he barked.

Like an obedient child, I didn't know what this was that he had on me, but I grabbed his hand and got up. Once I got myself together, I quickly grabbed my things I didn't even want to work out anymore.

"You ain't got to leave on my account. You just need to stop being a bitch when a nigga was just trying to help your rude ass," he voiced before leaving me standing there alone.

When he left out, I let out the breath I had been holding. Damn, it was something about him that had me gone in the head. I wasn't even fazed by his rude antics or the foul way he talked. I couldn't even focus on my work out because he had me distracted now.

Cutting off the treadmill, I headed out the door in hopes of catching up with him. I knew he lived in my building, but I just didn't know where.

Walking back to my building, I climbed the steps, and there he was standing at the door of the condo across from mine. When he saw me coming, he started to shake his head.

"Hey!" I called out to get his attention.

"I ain't trying to hear nothing you got to say," he replied. I jogged up the steps.

"No, wait. Look, I'm sorry I came off as rude last night, but you have to understand. Yes, I was drunk, so all I saw was a big ass nigga trying to hurt me. That was wrong of me. My name is Sherity," I voiced, holding my hand out for him to shake. He looked at my hand and then back at me.

Turning around, he closed the space between us.

"You're sorry, huh? You willing to make that up?" he mumbled. Lifting my brow in confusion, I opened my mouth to speak.

"Huh?"

"You willing to make up for all that smart-ass mouth you got?" he asked, looking behind me at my ass.

I had no clue where this was going, but him being this close to me had the seat of my panties soaking fucking wet.

"I got to get ready for work-k-k," I stuttered.

Even though he had sweated and worked out, the scent of

his body wash or cologne smelled so good. He pushed the door to his place open and pulled me inside. I couldn't move, so I stood like a statue in the middle of his floor. What the fuck was I doing? Half of me wanted this man to bend me over and break my back. Then the other side of me didn't know this man from a can of paint and this couldn't go down.

His strong hands moved to my waistband and jerked the Nike leggings I had on down to my ankles. It was nothing but silence in the room and my heavy breathing. He placed his hand in my back to lean me over on the edge of the couch. My body moved with no hesitation. His hand glided across my entrance.

"Damn, that shit leaking and fat," he moaned, and my pussy started to throb from the anticipation.

I could hear him fumbling with the condom wrapper. I looked over my shoulders. The way he licked his lips when our eyes met had me ready. This man was even finer in this moment. Where had he been all this time? I couldn't believe he had me in here being a hoe. He knew he was fine.

Once I felt him slide in with no warning, I let out the loudest moan.

"Ohhhhhhh!" I sighed. Jesus, it had been a minute since I had some dick, and he had *dick*. His thrusts had me fucking him back.

"Yeah, this exactly what I needed. Some good ass pussy," he moaned.

With his hands on my waist, we matched each other rhythm. Using my free hand, I started to thumb my clit. I felt him massaging my asshole with each thrust before he slipped his finger in my ass. Why did he do that? The euphoric feeling that it gave me had me gushing wet.

"Wet that shit up," he demanded. I couldn't even hold that shit in no more as I squirted all down my leg.

"Whoaa shit!" he moaned and pulled out.

"Turn over," he demanded, and I did as I was told, opening my legs to give him all access. The way he looked at my pussy and stroked his dick made me start back, thumbing my clit.

"Nah, let me handle that," he said, smacking my hand away.

He bent down and placed his mouth on my pussy. His warm tongue cascaded gently over my pearl. That along caught me off guard. I could tell he wasn't familiar with eating pussy, but the way that dick was hitting, I could overlook that shit. He looked up at me, and I held my gaze.

"I ain't never ate no pussy before, so don't talk no shit," he admitted.

He stood up and stroked his dick again before sliding back inside of me. *This nigga ain't never ate no pussy, so where the fuck he done been? Who don't eat pussy?* Each time he pushed himself inside of me, he stared at me, not breaking eye contact.

"You gone have to give me some more of this," he mumbled before releasing in the condom.

As soon as he walked off, I quickly started pulling my pants up, chastising myself for being a hoe. As soon as I was about to walk out the door, he rounded the corner.

"Damn, I was gone put you out first." He laughed, but I didn't find it funny.

"Look, this shit was fun, but it wasn't supposed to happen," I stated.

"Yeah, it probably wasn't supposed to, but it did, and you didn't stop it. You enjoyed it. You got some good pussy, so I forgive you for your rude ways." He winked.

I opened the door and was greeted by another fine ass man. *Choo choo went off in my head. Bitch get your shit together.*

"Damn, Don, you fucking the neighbor already?" he had the nerve to say. See, this was why I hated niggas.

I headed to my condo, doing a five-second walk of shame. As soon as I got inside and locked the door, I flew to the bathroom to shower and get ready for work.

CHAPTER 4

DON

I don't know what the hell came over me, but something about shorty and her smart-ass mouth turned me on. I was shocked that she even let me go as far as I did, but I needed that release. Watching her walk out the door, I had a smirk on my face because she just didn't know a nigga was finna be hitting that on the regular, and she lived across the hall.

Rubbing my hands over my head, I couldn't believe I put my mouth on her. I had never eaten pussy in my life, but I wanted to at least try. A nigga was gone have to work on that shit.

"My nigga, what the hell did I walk in on?" Loc asked.

"Shit, I had to find somebody to fuck since you fucked up last night with Sahara's dry ass," I replied.

"Ain't that shorty you cussed out last night, tho?"

"Yep and your point?" I headed to the bedroom so that I can hop in the shower.

"Shit, do you, player. I'm finna roll up!" Loc hollered from the living room.

Hoping in the shower, I took care of my hygiene and was ready to get my day started. After dressing and brushing my waves, I sprayed some cologne on and followed the potent scent of weed coming from the living room.

"What you got going today?" I asked Loc, grabbing the blunt from him.

"A meeting with Win and Kyelle, and then you know we got to hit the spot tonight for your official welcome home party," Loc spoke up.

"I'm gone roll to see moms first, then the warden got me the hookup on my driver's license, so the only thing I got to do is take the driver's test. You know that's a piece of cake," I told Loc as I took another hit of the blunt.

Flashbacks of the session I just had with shorty on the couch this morning caused a nigga mind to wander off. Sherity was her name, and that shit was etched in my brain.

"So, since you all over there in a daze, what was shorty across the hall hitting on?" Loc looked over at me.

"Man, shorty's pussy was so fye that it's gone be a fucking problem. She might have to move when I get done with her," I joked.

"Lies you tell. You just wait 'til all these hoes start throwing themselves at you at the club. You ain't even gone be thinking about her ass. She just convenient pussy." Loc smirked.

"I ain't worried about no hoe period. Ain't no love coming from my ass, and you know this shit."

"You say that now, no matter how hard you is the right person will come in and shut all that shit down," Loc laughed. Thinking about what he said, I knew that shit was a lie.

⬛ ⬛ ⬛ ⬛

I pushed the doorbell like I was crazy, knowing that it would piss my mama off.

"Whoever this is ringing my fucking doorbell like they crazy about to see me!" I could hear her yelling.

The door swung open, and the mug that she had displayed

on her face went to shocked and jumping in my arms.

"DonMir, oh my god baby what are you doing here?" she cried, touching me to make sure I was real.

"I wanted to surprise you with my release." I smiled.

Seeing her smile and not being able to contain her excitement made a nigga feel good. We walked into the house, and I closed the door behind me.

"You know you could've told me something hell I would've cooked. I know you hungry," she said.

"You can still cook, but I didn't want to get your hopes up because they were playing with a nigga's time," I lied a little.

"You got out today?"

"Nah, last night after midnight." I sighed, looking around the place. From the looks of it, the money that I was blessing her with over the years she remodeled the entire house.

"You like it?" she asked.

"It's not about if I like it, mama. This is your place you can do what you want to it," I told her and took off down the hallway to the room that used to be mine.

Opening the door, she still had some of my things in here, but it had been remodeled as well. The shit felt weird as hell being back in here after all these years. That's when it hit me, and I walked across the hall to my sister's room. Opening the door, I saw nothing had been touched. It was the same. Walking in, I could still smell her scent. My mother had touched nothing. Her room was the exact way she left it. A nigga heart felt like it was about to bust out my chest.

"I tried, but I just couldn't do it. Maybe since your home, we can do it together. That's if you want to," I heard my mother whisper behind me.

"It's time y'all let me go, it's okay I won't be mad," Donna spoke.

I tried my best to tune my sister out.

"Nah, we can keep it for a minute. I ain't ready," I admitted and walked out of her room.

"What you gone do with yourself since you out, Don?" my mother asked. I knew where this conversation was going, and she knew how I got down.

"Whatever I got to do and continue to make my money how I been making it." I shrugged, not really wanting to have this convo with her.

"Good, so you get out for murder but gone end up back in there for selling drugs and running these streets," she stated.

"Look, this all a nigga knows. I was in the streets before I got locked up, and the entire time I was behind bars, I made more than enough money to send to you to keep you out of debt and tried to buy you a new home. I run with big dogs, so I ain't gone be standing on no corners. I'm looking at a few investments and business ventures, but all that shit takes time. Please don't start with all that nagging!" I snapped and rubbed my temples.

"Didn't nobody ask you to throw your life away. You should've let the police handle that Don, so don't give me no sappy ass story," she had the nerve to say.

"Don't go there with mama, Don. Please don't," Donna's voice said.

"That was your motherfucking daughter out there laid in the fucking street beat and raped to a damn pulp, and you gone say some shit like that. I would've done the same shit for you. That nigga was walking around here like he ain't did shit. The police wouldn't have done shit. I ain't asking you to feel sorry for me because I'm good. I can't even believe you said this shit!" I barked, and the tears started to fall.

"Look, it has been twelve years, and Donna wouldn't want you out here acting like this," mom tried consoling me, but it was too late. Nobody knew that Donna was still here every step of the way with me. She wouldn't leave my head for shit.

"Yeah aite, I'm out," I told her and left my mother standing there. So much for that visit.

I hopped in the Audi and headed to the DMV. On the drive over, I looked over in the passenger seat, and there sat Donna shaking her head.

"I don't know why you're shaking your head," I mumbled.

"Because Don it was pointless, and she is still our mother. She just wants what is best for you. Look at her pain, as well. She didn't lose one but two children at the same time. No mother wants that. She doesn't care about all that monetary shit." Donna sighed.

"Yeah, aite."

"I want you to get some type of help. It's not healthy that you're holding on to me like this."

"You the one keep popping up and shit!" I snapped.

"You have me tucked away in your subconscious. So many things trigger your mental and brings me here. This shit doesn't look good if somebody pulls up beside you at the light and see you talking to yourself." Donna laughed.

"Fuck that. A nigga could be talking on a Bluetooth." I shrugged.

"Good luck on your test, baby brother." Donna smiled, then disappeared.

I pulled into the parking space and cut the engine. I texted the person that the warden told me to hit up so that I could let them know that I was here because I wasn't about to stand in this long ass line. When shorty came to the side door and flagged me down, I had to adjust my dick because her body was stacked as fucked. Shid, I knew I was about to pass this test with flying colors.

CHAPTER 5

SHERITY

E ntering my office, I picked up the new case file on my desk. Letting out a deep sigh, I hope it wasn't that deep of a case because, due to my caseload, I wanted a small breather. Taking a seat, I opened the chart and started to go over the file.

The beads of sweat that formed on my forehead dripped on the paper. My mouth grew dry as I could feel the vomit slowly trying to make its way out of my mouth. Being a social worker was my pride and joy, but sometimes things came across my desk that just triggered shit for me.

Scooting back, I grabbed a bottle of water out of my bag and took a swig. I had seen enough and had to get back on my shit.

A knock at my door pulled me from my thoughts.

"Come in!" I called out.

The door opened, and in walked my co-worker, Taylor. Taylor was a godsend. If I trusted anyone with my life, it was him.

"Bitch, how the fuck did you get home last night? You didn't even fucking answer the phone when I called!" he snapped.

Taylor was my homegirl trapped in a man's body. I didn't care what his preference was or how openly gay he was. He was all I had in a sense.

Taylor walked in and took a seat in the chair in front of me.

He looked at me right weird as if he were trying to figure something out.

"It's something different about you. Spill it hoe?" he smacked. *How in the hell could he tell anything?* Playing it off, I changed the subject.

"My ass went to sleep as soon as I got in last night. I was drunker than I thought," I partially lied.

Taylor stood from the chair and walked over to me. I followed him with my eyes as he leaned closer to me and had the nerve to sniff me.

"Oh, bitch, you got some dick." He gasped.

"Taylor, would you sit the hell down. I need someone to go to the home this child has been placed in and talk to her," I said, trying to divert the attention elsewhere.

"When did you start lying to me?" Taylor pouted, making me feel bad. Rubbing my temples, I let out a deep sigh.

"Ok, I had sex," I admitted. Taylor clapped his hands.

"Who was it?" he asked.

"I don't know, but it was a onetime thing," I replied, shutting it down. Taylor leaned back in his chair like he had passed out. He was so damn dramatic at times.

"Lawd my friend is a hoe, and I ain't know," he fake cried.

"Taylor, I'm not fooling with you. Please do what I asked about this case because this is a high alert case," I advised.

Taylor shook his head and grabbed the file. Looking at my computer, I tried to avoid the stares he was giving me.

"Don't think you getting out of giving me details. I want all the tea, and I prefer it hot with honey. Thank you," He smirked and exited my office.

Leaning on the desk, I thought about Don and how he handled me this morning. With the way that he put it down, it was no way that I couldn't think about that shit.

☐ ☐ ☐

Noon had come, and all I could think about was a margarita. After checking up on my caseload, everything was moving smoothly within the homes, and there were no problems. For the first time in a long time, I wasn't overworking myself. Closing my laptop, I got ready to head to lunch and check up on Taylor's ass.

Walking out of my office, I headed next door and knocked on Taylor's door before entering. Taylor was on the phone and held his finger up for me to hold on. Coming inside, I closed the door and stood there, eavesdropping on the conversation.

"Yes, ma'am, okay, thank you. You can expect a home visit since you can't make it into the office. We just need to talk to her. It's a check-up into her claim," Taylor spoke. While Taylor finished up his call, I looked at my watch.

"You ready to go?" He sighed.

"Is everything okay with that case?" I asked. Taylor rolled his eyes.

"I see now why you had me look over it. You sure you okay to work on this one. I'll take the entire thing if you want me to." He sighed and touched me on my shoulder.

"You can take it. I really don't need that on my plate. If you need help, though, I got you," I told him. Taylor and I gathered our things and left the office for lunch. We walked across the street to the Mexican restaurant.

"So, tell me about this piece of dick you got sis, and I want to know everything," Taylor whispered as we walked to our table and got seated. Sliding into the booth, I grabbed the menu and placed my drink order.

"It was my neighbor, and the only thing I know about him is his name is Don, and he's rude as hell." I sighed.

"Wait a minute, so how did this come about, and as many times I've been to your house, I never knew of this neighbor."

"I honestly think he just moved in because no one has lived across the hall from me in a minute."

"Oh, he lives across the hall, huh?" Taylor looked at me crazy.

"That don't mean shit, but anyway, I cussed him out last night when I got home. You know I was drunk, so this morning, I wake up thinking I'm about to start a fresh day go work out and shit. When I get to the gym, I start my workout, and this fine ass man came out of the sauna dripping in sweat. We had words again, basically him cussing me out about the night before and storms out. I felt bad, so I decided to go apologize, and things went in a different direction.

Taylor, he pulled me into his condo, and Jesus, he worked me like I ain't never been worked before. I ain't never had dick like that in my life," I sighed and propped my head in my hands.

"Oh, sweet Lord, you is whipped," he shook his head. I wasn't worried about what he was talking about.

"Whatever you wait till you see him, well, if you ever get to see him," I shrugged. Somebody's birthday was taking place, and I watched as the team members walked over to the person's table and started singing and carrying on. I covered my ears and closed my eyes.

"Sherity, do you want to leave?" Taylor whispered.

"No, there is no way that I will let that shit get to me," I snapped. Today was the birthday of someone that I absolutely despised. That's why I been drinking so much.

"Okay, I was just making sure."

⬚ ⬚ ⬚

"Taylor, what the hell are you doing?" I asked, walking into the living room, fully dressed and ready to go. Taylor was peeping out of the peephole.

"Just watching this door in hopes of seeing your mystery dick," he smirked. When he turned around, his mouth hit the floor.

"Bitch I thought we were going to happy hour; do I need to change?" he asked. I only had on a black cocktail dress, but it was snug and showcased my slim fit and ass.

"Taylor hush this dress isn't even all that. Plus, change of plans no happy hour. It's a new spot that I heard about that I want to try out," I smirked.

"No, ma'am, you not about to play me. Why you get to get all razzle dazzled, and I don't even get the option. You lucky I keep shit in my car," he smacked and headed toward the door, following him to the door.

I stood in the breezeway, cracking up at him as he cussed all the way to the car. That's when it hit me, that unique smell that I would remember in a room full of men. I looked at his door, and he must have either just went in or came out because he left his scent lingering. Taylor made his way back up the steps, and halfway loud laughter and the door opening of Don's condo caught both of our attention. Don and the guy that came earlier this morning exited the condo. Don and I locked eyes, and he gave me a look taking me in from head to toe. Taylor came and stood beside me.

"Bitch, which one is it?" he whispered, and I tapped him in his stomach, trying to make him hush. Don smirked at me and locked his door.

"I mean damn somebody gone say something everybody just looking and shit!" Don barked, breaking the silence.

"Why is your mouth so foul? How you doing?" I said to Don but held my hand out for his friend.

"Shit, I'm straight. What's your name?" he asked and shook my hand.

"Sherity and yours?"

"You can call me Loc," he replied.

"This is my friend, Taylor. Well, nice meeting you Loc, you're not mean like your friend," I smirked.

"Whatever come on bruh ain't nobody trying to hear all that shit," he mumbled. This man was a piece of work, and it just amazed me how much of an ass he was.

"Wheww, chile," Taylor sang and walked back in the house. I followed suit and looked back at Don when he got to the bottom of the steps, he looked back at me and winked. *Now, what kind of shit was that?*

CHAPTER 6

DON

When we hopped in the car, Loc was looking at me like he wanted to say something. I started the car and pretended as if he wasn't. Sherity was looking fine as hell in that dress.

"My nigga you know I don't care how you come off at me, but I know you're feeling shorty across the hall," Loc said, looking at me.

Shaking my head, I just laughed at this nigga. I could honestly say I wasn't feeling her; she just had some good pussy.

"Nigga, how you come up with that because ain't nobody feeling shit. I wouldn't mind feeling them walls again, and that's about it," I admitted.

"Sherity, I can see you calling her SheShe or some shit." He laughed.

"Dude, fuck you!" I barked.

The night was young, and I was ready to turn up and celebrate. I got my license, so that shit was a celebration within itself. I never got around to meeting Win today because some shit came up and he had to leave the state, but my time was coming. When we pulled up to the club, the lot was packed. Whipping my car in front of the club, I handed my keys to the valet attendant. Loc hopped out and put his hat on his head. Dressed in all black, I slid my Versace frames on my face and adjusted my chain.

The sounds of Rod Wave's "Rags to Riches" was blaring through the speakers. It was a laid-back vibe not on no rah-rah shit, so I nodded in approval because I could relax a little. Loc guided us to the section that we had reserved. As soon as we sat down, a few girls swarmed us and took our order. A nigga wanted some chicken wings and shrimp with a big ass bottle of Rémy. My eyes landed on this shorty that was posted up right outside of VIP. Glancing down at her ass, that motherfucker was big and sitting up nice. She waved and signaled for me to come to her. I ain't really want nobody up here with me because I wasn't on that type of shit. I stood up and walked over to the bar and leaned over.

"You don't remember me, do you?" she asked. I lifted my brow to get a better look at her.

"Nope, am I supposed to, shorty?" I asked.

"We went to school together. I know you been gone all this time. Sorry about your sister," she said, looking away. For some reason, her bringing up my sister just didn't sit well with me.

"Aw yeah thanks, but I don't remember you, though," I said and headed back to my seat. Quickly I poured me up a drink and took it to the head.

As the night went on a nigga was feeling good and the Rémy had me vibing. I was up to date on all the new music because I had it like that while locked up.

"I'm finna go piss!" I yelled over the music to Loc. Making my way through the crowd, I kept my eyes on these mother-fuckers that I knew nothing about. When I looked up, this little bitty ass nigga was glaring at me like he had a problem. I really wasn't stuttin' his ass, but he was blocking where I needed to pass.

"'Cuse me, bruh," I said so that I could get by.

"I see they let your ass out," he mugged. One thing about me I didn't take disrespect well, and I felt disrespected like a motherfucker.

"Nigga, who the fuck is you?" I asked, walking up on him.

"Don't worry about all that, but you better watch your back. That shit you pulled, don't forget he had homies too," the smurf had the nerve to say. I let out a small chuckle.

"Am I supposed to be scared, little nigga? I will toss your ass across this damn club and not think twice about it. I don't take threats lightly so you and your homies can bring whatever you want to bring because I guarantee it will be the last time you do that shit, fuck boy!" I snapped and bumped the dude so hard he hit the floor, and folks started laughing.

Shaking my head, I couldn't believe they sent the smallest nigga out with the threat. Now, I was gone have to find out who the fuck he was because he had to see me outside of witnesses.

As soon as I got done taking a piss, I headed to the patio area so I could smoke this blunt because dude had me ready to go back to jail. I knew that being released, I might run into somebody that was affiliated with that nigga, but it is what it is. Removing the blunt from behind my ear, I lit that bitch and took a big ass toke.

Turning around, I scanned the patio, and I saw the dude that was with Sherity walk out and start looking around. His eyes landed on me, and I quickly turned around.

"Hey, Don, right?" he asked.

"You don't know me, bruh," I replied.

"I was just about to ask had you seen Sherity? I went to the bathroom and told her to stand by the door because she had a few drinks, and I can't find her ass," he hissed. I hit the blunt and blew the smoke in his face.

"Why the fuck your gal always drunk, and nah, I ain't seen her?" He stood there for a few seconds. I was really waiting on him to answer my question, but he walked off instead. Finishing off the blunt, I scanned the parking lot from the patio. I had a good ass view of my ride in valet and just peeped the scene.

"Aye, shorty come on, my homie and me gone take you home," I heard some dude say.

"Nooo, I'm waiting on my bestie," the girl moaned.

I turned around to see two niggas hovering over Sherity. She was gone off her ass. They both stood on the side of her holding her arms up as she was trying to keep that short ass dress she wore down. They left the patio area, and I shook my head but followed behind them.

See, this damn girl was gone get her fucking ass killed all this damn drinking. I pulled my phone out and shot Loc a text letting him know wassup and to meet me outside. These niggas were looking like Ice Cube and the other dude on *The Players Club* when they were trying to take Ebony out of the club.

As soon as we exited the club and they got to the parking lot, Loc was already at my side.

"Sherity!" I called out. The dudes stopped and looked back at me

"I think y'all need to let the lady go. She's with me," I spoke with authority. I started to walk toward them. I signaled for Loc to get Sherity.

"Man, nigga, she said she was coming with us, so she ain't with you no more." One of the guys laughed. In a flash, I removed my gun from my waistband and had it to his head.

"Let her go, and I promise you I'm not gone repeat myself!" I spat through gritted teeth.

The dude let Sherity go, and Loc grabbed her. I took the gun and went across his face with the butt of it while his homeboy took off running with his pussy ass. I turned to Sherity, who was now throwing up. Marching over to her, I grabbed her by her arm.

"Why the fuck yo ass always drunk and shit. You were about

to leave with them niggas shorty, and your ass would've ended up on the side of the road somewhere dead!" I yelled.

"Stop, you're hurting me," she cried. This girl had me hot.

"Man, where the fuck your keys and your phone at?"

She just stood there, not saying shit. I ripped the purse she had around her off the fucking straps and opened it to retrieve her phone and keys.

"Unlock this motherfucker and call your friend. He's looking for you," I demanded. She quickly grabbed her phone and then handed it to me while she started throwing up again.

"Aye, come to the parking lot. I found Sherity," I told him and hung up.

"You gone take her home?" Loc asked. I just looked at her looking pitiful as hell. Why the fuck was she doing this shit to herself?

"Yeah, I'm gone get her friend to bring her car to her house," I told him.

"Word let me go back in here and handle this little business, and I get up with you later. I'm gone catch a ride with this little shorty to my ride."

"Aite," I told him and dapped him up. By that time, Sherity's friend had made it out of the club.

"Oh my god, Sherity, I was looking for you!" he yelled. Rolling my eyes, I let out an irritated sigh.

"Man, she was on some drunk shit and almost got that ass handed to her by two niggas she ain't know. Take her car to the crib, and I'm gone bring her home," I instructed.

Pulling Sherity by her arm, I dragged her ass to the car. Once inside, she laid back in the seat. When I got in, I just looked at her. Even in a drunken stupor, she was still beautiful, and she had me so damn mad. Starting the car, I looked over at her.

"You throw up in my car, and that's your ass," I threatened.

CHAPTER 7

SHERITY

My fucking head was spinning, and I just wanted to lie in my bed. I didn't even have a lot to drink, so I'm not understanding what the fuck is going on. Taylor and I both only had two drinks when we got here because we skipped happy hour. Turning my head, I glanced over and noticed Don driving. The angry look on his face made him so sexy. I could feel my body getting hot, and I don't know what it was, but I got extremely horny. Then YFN Lucci's "Wet" came on, and Lord, that song does something to me. I used my hand to move to his lap.

"Man, keep your little drunk ass over there. This ain't that," he said, smacking my hand away. I took my hand and slowly lifted my dress, showcasing the Fenty underwear that I had on. Moving my panties to the side, I slid my fingers inside of me, and I could feel Don staring at me.

"I don't know what it is, but my body is so hot, and I want you inside of me," I whimpered.

"Did you take something, man?" he asked as we sat at the red light. I removed the seat belt and placed my hands back in lap and started to undo his pants. His breathing picked up, and I know he wanted to resist.

"Man, shorty, you on some other shit," he moaned.

Once I had his dick in my hands, I placed him inside of my

mouth. Once his dick was in my mouth, all that shit he was talking ceased. He drove on while I continued to give him the best head I ever gave anybody. Once I felt his hand rest on top of my head, I knew he was feeling this shit. I made love to that nigga's dick the entire time the song played.

"Shit I'm about to nut," he said, I continued to suck until I felt him release in my mouth. Now I wanted to hop on.

"Pull over," I moaned.

"Man, hell nah, sit yo hot pussy ass down we almost at the crib. You sure you ain't take nothing? What all you have to drink and don't lie?" he looked at me. No matter how hard he tried to be, I could see a soft side within him.

"I don't do drugs. For one, I work for the fucking state, and Taylor and I only had two drinks. Then those guys came over and started keeping me company. They were cool," I sighed, trying to remember everything.

"Them niggas probably slipped something in your drink without you knowing," he said.

The car stopped and looking out the window we were at home. Don got out and made his way over to my side of the car, where he opened the door.

"Can you walk?" he asked. I nodded my head yes and stood up. Right away, everything started to spin, and I grabbed ahold of the car door.

"Man, come on," Don said, closing the door, then lifting me in his arms.

With my arms wrapped tightly around his neck, I placed my face in the crook of his neck, inhaling the cologne that was teasing me. As we walked up the steps, I pecked his neck with my lips.

"Sherity, stop before I drop your ass," he mumbled.

"I don't have my keys to get into my condo," I whispered.

"Taylor's got your keys, you staying at my crib," he said.

Slowly placing me down, I leaned against the wall as he removed his keys and unlocked the door. Picking me back up, he carried me inside and closed the door with his foot. We walked down a long hallway that led to his bathroom. Placing me in the chair at the end of his bed, he walked off to the bathroom, where I heard the shower turn on. I tried my best to remove my shoes but just couldn't get it together.

Don entered the room and removed my shoes.

"Stand up," he demanded, and I did. "Take this shit off," he said, tugging at my dress.

He had me so wet that I knew my pussy juices were running down my leg. Once my dress hit the floor, we stood looking at each other.

"Go get in the shower," he said and smacked me on the ass.

I couldn't walk at first, but somehow, I got some strength in my legs to get to the shower and wash the night's funk off of me. I was anticipating all the things that were about to take place once I got out.

After my shower, I felt a bit better, but I was still horny. Grabbing the towel, I wrapped it around my body and walked back to the bedroom. There was a t-shirt on the bed, so I grabbed and threw on. The room was silent, but I heard talking in the front, so I headed toward the living room. When I entered the living room, Don was closing the door and placing keys on the table. When he saw me standing there, he looked at me and shook his head — typical Don.

"That was your friend bringing your keys. He said he would call you tomorrow," he told me.

"Thank you for everything tonight," I told him. Don took a seat on the couch, and I walked over to him and sat down beside him.

"Don't thank me. I just don't like to see niggas taking advantage of women. When you said you worked for the state, what do you do?" he asked.

"I'm a social worker. Love helping those that don't have a voice." I smiled.

"You know they say first impressions are everything and let's just say based on yours and the shit I saw tonight. You like to party, huh?" he asked. I swallowed the lump that formed in my throat. He was starting to get too personal.

"I just like to unwind after the long days I have. It's draining and sometimes a lot for one to take in the things that a lot of the kids go through at home," I partially lied.

"Yeah, aite, I know you lying," he mumbled.

"How do you know I'm lying when you don't even know me?"

"It's just something I picked up over the years, and I know when someone isn't truthful," he looked at me. I looked away because his stare became uncomfortable.

"My name is Sherity, and I'm twenty-six years old. I'm a social worker, and I have one friend, and that's Taylor. I have no family because they disowned me, so yes, I drink a little more than I should to cope with things." I shrugged. At this point, I didn't care what the hell he knew.

"Why your family disown you?" he looked at me.

"Now that I will not get into. Here I am telling you all about me, and you still a mystery," I replied.

"Gone stay a mystery too," he said and licked his lips. The way his pink tongue glided across his lips in slow motion. Had me getting aroused again.

"That's fine, at this point, I just want some dick," I blurted out and said. I lifted my shirt and climbed in his lap. Don's hands cuffed my ass. Slowly he lifted me while I grabbed his dick and found its way to my entrance. As I came down, a soft moan escaped my lips.

"Fuck girl, yeah, they had to give you something because you weren't this wet earlier," Don stated and bit down on his lip as I started to move up and down. I was moving slowly because this shit was spreading me out, and I was still a little sore from this morning.

"Nah, you were begging for this dick, so you better take this shit!" Don barked and smacked me on my ass.

The sting that came from that caused me to jump and pick up the pace. The wetter I got, the faster I started to go. I don't know what came over me, but I rode that nigga like it was no tomorrow.

"Shit, I'm about to cum!" I cried out.

"You better hold that shit!" he spat back and placed his hands around my neck.

"Harder," I moaned, and his grip got a little tighter, and his stroke got a little faster.

"You gone catch this nut?" he whispered in my ear. I nodded my head, yes.

"Get down there!" he barked, and I hopped off the dick and got on my knees, welcoming his kids.

CHAPTER 8

DON

Glancing over at Sherity, I ran my hands across my chest and shook my head. This was the ultimate no-no for a nigga. I let this girl spend the night and get inside of my head. For some reason, I was really trying to figure her out. It was a lot about her that was mysterious we were too much alike. She didn't look like that type that a family would disown, and that continued to play in my head as well.

Sherity popped up so fast and then looked at me. My eyes landed on her exposed breasts.

"Oh my god, what time is it. I can't be late for work," she started to panic.

"You do know it's Saturday, right?" I mumbled. I could tell she released a sigh of relief.

"Thank god, but still, I need to head home. Thank you for coming to my aid last night because you didn't have to. I guess you're not so mean after all." She smiled and slid out of bed gathering her things from last night.

"I will wash and return your shirt," she said. I nodded my head and watched as she left the bedroom. Once I heard the door closed, I slid out of bed and went to lock it back.

"As hard as you're trying not to baby brother, you like that girl," Donna spoke.

"You never was the one to mind your business," I told her as I looked at my sister.

"You two need each other in a way that you have no clue about. I can't say much, but once you figure it out, you will see everything come full circle. Be careful with her. She is damaged goods," Donna smiled.

There was no need to tell me to be careful with her because I wasn't going to bother her. Shit, at the rate things were going, I might have to stop fucking her ass too because I don't want to send any mixed signals to her.

"I know what you're thinking, and I don't care what you say. I will have the last laugh," she said and vanished.

It was time for me to get on with my day. I was finally meeting up with Win today, and I needed to check on my shit at the jail. After handling my hygiene, I texted Loc to get the address for the meeting so I could put in the GPS. After locking up, I headed to the other part of town. I was ready to get my hands dirty out here in the streets and do whatever I needed to do on top of running my crew. The money that I had put up I was going to open something up just didn't know what exactly.

About thirty minutes later, I pulled up to this big ass crib. As soon as I pulled in the gate, the variety of cars let me know this nigga was paid. I spotted Loc truck sitting in the cut.

Once parked, I got out and made my way to the entrance, where I rang the doorbell. This shit was phat and motivated the hell out of me. The door opened, and an older lady greeted me.

"May I help you?" she asked.

"Yes, I'm here to meet Win, he is expecting me," I answered.

"That's my nigga Mahdea let him in," Loc hollered. The lady moved to the side and I dapped up Loc and followed him.

"We outside. You came just in time," Loc spoke. Once we stepped outside, it was a few other cats out there. I assume the big nigga with dreads was Win. Some badass chick sat in his lap.

"DonMir Telhide," he spoke and tapped the lady on her thigh, signaling for her to get up. Once she got up, he made his way over to me. Holding his hand out, I gave him a solid shake.

"Mi finally get to meet the one bringing mi in a lot of money," he spoke.

"Man, I appreciate you putting me on and letting me do that for you," I told him.

"Thank Loc, he is a good friend," Win stated.

Once I looked behind him, I saw this small ass nigga walking up, and instantly my mood changed. I guess Win saw the look on my face, so he turned to see what I was looking at.

"Is there a problem?"

"Hell yeah, I don't fuck with that little nigga, and I'm two seconds off his ass for threatening me last night!" I spat. Win looked around at everyone.

"You com'mere!" he barked, pointing to the dude. He made his way over to us.

"What's the problem? He's with me," some other guy spoke up.

"My guest is not feeling your friend. What reason is that?" Win asked, facing to me.

"I assume he affiliated with the nigga I murdered. Like I give a fuck," I spat.

"Is this true?" he turned to the nigga I was mugging.

"If it is?" he had the nerve to ask.

"You're fired and you too if you have a problem as well," Win flat out spoke. I started to laugh because both them niggas was speechless, but I could tell they wouldn't dare speak on that shit.

"My beef ain't with you, Win," one guy spoke.

"It may not be, but it is with my soldier. You mad because he murdered a rapist, that right there tells me all I need to hear. You are dismissed," Win said, shooing them both away.

"I'm sure I'll catch up to you around the way and trust I'm not done!" I spat.

The two of them left out, and Win handed me a glass filled with brown liquor.

"Sit down and relax. Don, this is my wife, Kyelle," he introduced us. I had heard about her. She was a female hustler that was over the Kandi Lane shit and had her own brand of weed. I nodded my head.

"Now that you are home, what do you want to do?" Win asked.

"I got a crew that will run the streets, plus I still want re-ups for the jails. The warden is already on board. The money I have made I want to invest in something but I'm just not sure yet. I was thinking about a moving company, get a few trucks. It's just a thought, though," I shrugged.

"A thought but a good idea. I will hook you up with my business guy. You can discuss the things with him, and he will legit handle everything you need. You just tell him the ideas, numbers, and all that other shit," Win stated.

I nodded my head.

"Everyone on our team eats, and we don't do wars. Now I know that shit that just happened might bring some heat back out, but I need you out here and not back in jail. Handle your shit discreetly or get someone else to handle it. Don't you ever let a motherfucker tell you what you did was wrong because, as a man, I would've done the same thing for my wife," Win stated. I didn't give a fuck about what anybody said because I knew what the fuck I was doing, and that was that.

"I hear ya," I told him and took a sip from my cup.

❏ ❏ ❏

As the day went on, I sat back and observed a lot of things about this man and his organization. The way that he let his wife do her own thing and he loved on her was a first for me. Coming up, I never witnessed my father or any man love on my mama correctly. Then the same thing with my sister, she was betrayed by someone that she loved. Love wasn't a fit in my life. Win proved all you need is to have someone that matched you on a level that only y'all understood. Even though both of them were equal and led the same, it wasn't a power trip for either one of them. They were equally yoked. That's when my thoughts went to Sherity. She was still a mystery, but who was I to bring my baggage into her world, and it was clear she had a lot of baggage she was carrying to.

❏ ❏ ❏

The ride back to my crib, as I stopped by the wing place that was next door so I could grab some food, my phone rang. Looking at the caller ID it was my right hand back in the jam.

"Yo, what it do?" I answered.

"Just letting you know that I got my package. You good, tho?" he asked, which caused me to perk up.

"What you mean, am I good?"

"You know shit travels fast. That nigga Toolie said he had some folks out there trying to get at you," he mentioned.

"I'm straight. Ain't shit that I can't handle. Hit me when it's gone," I told him, referring to my supply. I needed to find out how the fuck dude was connected to Toolie. I knew this shit had his name all over it.

Hopping out the car, I walked into the wing spot. After placing my order for a 10-piece extra crispy lemon pepper with special sauce and peach Kool-Aid, I grabbed my ticket and stood off to the side.

"Dang, I should've put my food on your tab," I heard, looking up into the eyes of Sherity.

"Sup SheShe," I spoke then had to laugh at myself because Loc and what he said popped up into my head.

"Ohhh SheShe, I got a nickname." She flashed that pretty ass smile of hers. Sherity was beautiful as hell. I usually was attracted to the light skin type, but she was the same complexion as me, and she just had this glow about her all the time. The honey-golden hair she had in a bob cut looked perfect with her skin tone. She was rocking a yellow sundress and had them toes out. I couldn't find shit wrong with this girl.

"Don't look too hard into a nickname," was all I said. She stood beside me and leaned against the wall.

"How long you been here?" I asked.

"Shit, about ten minutes. It's worth the wait though they wings be fye." She smiled.

"Why you got your ass out?" I asked and found myself sliding my hand behind her.

"My ass isn't out. You jealous?" She smirked

"Wassup, Don?" another voice said, and I looked up.

I swear I didn't know ole gal, but it was the one from the club last night. I didn't even speak. I just hit her with a nod. She looked at Sherity with a weird look then back at me.

"Number 15!" the people called, and Sherity pushed herself off the wall.

"That's me," she looked at me and said. She started to walk off, but before she did, she turned back around and looked at me.

"I'll see you at home," she smiled and winked. I caught all that shit she was throwing. Gal tried to come over here and blow up our spot, but little did she know Sherity had that shit on lock. I had no plans of linking with her tonight, so I just played along.

"You just make sure she hot and ready," I said with a straight face.

"Y'all cute. I saw y'all leave the club together last night. So that's your girl?" she asked. Why in the fuck was shorty all in my personal business.

"You all in a nigga business, and I don't even know you," I sighed.

"I know enough about you, and the fact that both of y'all are together is weird as fuck. Ain't no way," she said, smacking her teeth. I leaned off the wall.

"Why is me being with her weird?" She had my attention now.

"I'm saying I just couldn't be with the person that killed my brother." She sighed. When she said that it felt like someone had sucked the life out of me. I pulled her close to me.

"The fuck is you talking about?" I said through gritted teeth.

"You ain't know Sherity is Rasheed sister. Damn, you must don't remember shit from back then," she said, yanking away from me.

I had to play it off.

"I know who the fuck she is, I was testing your ass because you seem to be all in a nigga business. Don't worry about what we got going on," I told her.

"Number 16!" they called out, and that was my number. Looking at her like she was crazy, I left her standing there and grabbed my food. Leaving out the restaurant, I couldn't get in my truck quick enough.

Thinking back, I really didn't know that he had a sister. With her being younger than me, we should've gone to school together. I don't remember her from school. I would've known all this shit. I wonder did she know who the hell I am.

"Before you jump to conclusions, don't count her out just yet. Things are just now coming to light. Remember, I told you that y'all had similar stories. Don't let her get away. Everything will be revealed soon," Donna's voice hit me.

Starting the truck, I backed out and headed home. I had to do the only other thing I could think of and call Loc. While the phone rang, I just kept letting what gal say replay in my head. When Loc's voice came over the speaker, it broke me from that.

"Sup nigga!" he answered.

"Aye, did Rasheed have a sister?" I asked.

"Shit, I don't remember if he did or not. That nigga had mad shorty's around him on the regular, so I can't remember why wassup?" Loc asked.

"I ran into this shorty at the wing spot and SheShe was there,"

"SheShe my nigga, what I tell you," he laughed.

"Fuck you, but nah forreal. While she and I were talking, this gal that claims she went to school with me walked up so when SheShe walked off. She was like are y'all together if so that's weird. So, I'm like why is that she said some shit like she couldn't be with the person who killed her brother. Basically, saying Sherity was Rasheed's sister." I sighed.

"That's some deep shit. Do you think she knows who you are?"

"I don't know she's got a lot of shit going on with her she so secretive, but I wouldn't know because she ain't acting no type of way. I got to figure out a way to ask her about this shit," I replied.

"Well, good luck with that shit. Hit me when you find out. I'm out to get my dick sucked," Loc laughed. I shook my head.

"Bye nigga!" I said and ended the call.

CHAPTER 9
SHERITY

The vibe at the wing spot was totally different from Don, and I wasn't expecting that. Nor was I complaining. I did decide to play along when gal came over there, trying to make herself known. I remember her from school, but I never was the one to hang around her or her circle. Don may have been playing, but I would seriously be knocking on his door later.

For the first time in years, I had felt something for a man. Regardless if it was just sex, I had never allowed myself to get the way that Don had me. He had me open, and in a weird needy way, he made me feel safe. Placing my food on the table, I removed my shoes and went to get out of my clothes. Slipping into my pajama dress, I was ready to stuff my face and watch me something on Netflix.

Hopping on the couch, I grabbed my food and started to tear it down. Once I got to the second chicken wing, there was a knock at my door. Pausing the TV, I walked to the door and looked out the peephole. On the other end was Don, and he was looking dead at me. Slowly I opened the door, and he stood there holding his food.

"Wassup, your girlfriend let you leave?" I asked, moving away from the door to let him in.

He didn't even respond; he just sat his food on the table and got comfortable. Locking the door, I got back in my spot and hit play on the TV and continued to eat my food.

Everything was silent. All you could hear was chewing and the damn TV. Once I had enough, I placed the plate back on the table on wiped my mouth. Looking at Don, he had a lost look on his face.

"You good?" I asked him. He closed his plate and let out a deep sigh.

"Just got some shit on the brain," he answered.

"You want to talk about it?"

"Shit, do you want to talk about it?" he shot back. I was a bit confused.

"What are we supposed to be talking about?" he was starting to make me uncomfortable, so I shifted a bit.

"Why are you so nervous all of a sudden? Look, this is not usually the way I roll, but you spoke on some things, and it kind of left me wanting to know more about you," he had the nerve to say. Ok, it must be about to snow in the middle of summer.

"Some things are too delicate to just discuss with anyone. We don't even know each other like that to be going so deep, don't you think?"

"If that were the case, I wouldn't have asked you. I really just want to know why your family disowned you. You seem like a pretty decent chick." I just looked at him because he was really about to make me open up this can of worms.

"I will tell you, but you have to tell me something about you, deal?" I asked.

"Aite," he nodded.

"When I was fourteen, my brother was murdered for doing the unthinkable to a girl. My brother death didn't faze me at all. I was thrilled and happy that someone had removed him from my life. They helped me escape a pain that I had been trying to escape for years. Of course, my family tried to downplay and say that it was just rumors, but I knew the truth, and I believed he did everything that they said he did to that poor girl. I waited until I was sixteen to come out to my family about my truth. I remember the look on my mother's face when I told her that my brother had been messing with me since I was twelve. I hated my brother for invading my privacy and taking my innocence no matter how it was done. He was nasty, and that shit was sick. I always thought my brother was my protector, but once he started touching me and doing things to me, I wanted him dead. Anyway, my mother cussed me out and called me all kinds of fast ass hoes for lying on the deceased.

On my seventeenth birthday, we were all celebrating me going off to college, but I was still hurting. My brother messed up my relationships and outlook I had on men. So, while everyone was there, I told all they asses about they nasty ass son, nephew, cousin. My mother was so embarrassed she told me to get the fuck out. When I left, I found out she had blocked me, and when my friends would go by, she would tell them that she didn't have a daughter.

"I later found out she had got into my granny's head as well, and it was to the point that all my other family members just turned their nose up at me and did the same. I went on to college and pushed myself through. I had no friends or nobody. Taylor is the only person that knows about my past well you now. Throughout college, I started to live this double life. By day I was the model student, and at night it was like all the pain came back, and I used drinking to numb it. As you probably know that I still kind of do that now." I sighed and wiped the tears that attempted to fall. Don sat there, and I could tell he was pissed.

"That's some fucked up shit not to have your family believe you or be in your corner when you needed them. So, you were happy that nigga got murked?"

"I know it might sound bad, but he got what he deserved. If he did that shit to me and then the girl that he claimed to love, ain't no telling how many other girls he did that shit to. I just never saw that shit coming."

"It makes you think, but I went to jail for murder. That's my secret. I actually just got out that night that you saw me," Don stated, and I could tell that he was still in a trance.

"Who did you murder?"

"Nobody really if you asked me, but I proudly did my time." He shrugged.

"I just told you my darkest secret, and you're just giving me the key points to your life." I was slightly irritated. Don hopped up and grabbed his things.

"I know I'm sorry, and I plan on telling you more, but I got to go," he stated.

"Did I say something wrong?"

"No, you didn't so don't think that. I got to go," he said again and rushed out the door. I jumped at the slamming of the door and fell back on the couch. What the fuck just happened?

CHAPTER 10

SHERITY

Two Months Later

Peeking through the blinds, I watched as Don backed his work truck in. It was nice to see that he appeared to be doing good for himself since we haven't talked since the night he stormed out of here. I admit I'm still a bit confused, but it was out of my hands. I just couldn't figure out what went wrong. When he looked up at my window, I closed the blinds quickly and moved away from the window.

There was no way that he hasn't thought about me because he had been on my mind ever since. I grabbed my things and got ready to head out because I was meeting Taylor for drinks. At one point, I had slowed down on the drinking, but it didn't last long. Opening the door, I stepped out and caught Don's friend Loc exiting his place.

"Sup, SheShe!" he spoke.

"Hey Loc," I mumbled I wasn't in the mood to really speak.

"Damn why you sound like that?" he asked as we walked down the steps.

"No reason, just hoping not to run into your boy," I admitted.

"You miss him, don't you? I told that nigga y'all miss each other." He laughed. That caught me off guard.

"Excuse me?"

"He walking around meaner than he was," Loc whispered.

"Well, I have nothing to do with that. He ghosted me one night, and I haven't heard shit from him. You know what's fucked up, it was right after I confided in him about something really sentimental to me. If I had known he was going to act like this, I would've kept it to myself and stayed the fuck away from him!" I yelled.

"Yo!" Don's voice boomed at us. When I locked eyes with him if looks could kill, he would've been dead. I turned on my heels and headed to my car. Fuck him.

When I got in the car, I couldn't understand the emotions that were going through me. Placing my head on the steering wheel, I couldn't believe that I was allowing tears to fall for some-one that could give two shit about me.

TAP! TAP!

The knocking on the window caused me to look up. When I looked up, Don was standing there with the meanest scowl on his face.

"Let the window down!" he barked. My first instinct was to start my car and pull off on his ass, then the other half of me wanted to hear what he had to say. I turned the car on so that I could roll the window down.

"What, Don?" I sighed.

"Where the hell you going SheShe and don't lie?" he had the nerve to ask.

"The last time I checked, we haven't talked in two months since you remember that night you ran out on me. So, you don't have any rights on what I'm about to do!" I snapped. Don looked at me and let out a deep sigh.

"Look Loc told me about y'all conversation, and I just didn't want you to be drinking and shit," he said. I couldn't contain my laughter.

"It's a little late for that you have contributed to an increase in that shit. You know what you at least owe me an explanation on what the hell happened." Don stood up and placed his hands on top of his head. I could tell he was conflicted.

"That's what I thought. Bye Don!" I spat and rolled the window up just as quickly. I hit reverse so fast, trying to back up out of that parking lot. Looking in the rearview, Don just stood there, shaking his head.

🞍 🞍 🞍

When I got to the bar, Taylor was sitting there waiting with my drink already ordered. As soon as I sat down, I grabbed the glass and took the biggest gulp.

"Honey child, what the hell happened that you called all in a damn frenzy?" Taylor immediately went in.

"Don, who the fuck else?" I snapped and took another sip.

"I wish y'all just kiss and make up already because you got it bad. I thought you were done with him. I told you about spying on him," he rambled.

"I wasn't spying on him, Taylor. I had a conversation with Loc, and word got back to him. He was so concerned about my drinking habit that he happened to finally speak to me after two months," I partially lied.

"I don't know what prompted the disappearance, but it's clear that cares about you. You were doing good cutting back, and you shouldn't let anybody get you back to that place. I don't care how healthy you think you are all this drinking is going to catch up with you. You can't continue to go through life numbing yourself. Your brother is gone, and you should've been done got some type of professional help to help you get through that, sis. Look before you bite my head off, I'm just telling you this because I love you and I wouldn't be any kind of friend if I didn't say something. I'm worried about you, Sherity." Taylor sighed as he scooted his chair close to me.

I couldn't even be mad at him for his truth.

"I just want to forget it and push it back to this space in my head that I never have to revisit, but somehow it just manages to pop out like hey I'm here," I cried and tossed the remainder of the drink back.

"Your life ain't all that bad if you look at it from the out-side. You have a great career; you own your own shit. All you need is a man and have some babies you'll be set, friend. I'm just scared."

"Well, after one more drink, I might make that change," I lied. I heard everything that Taylor was saying, but the way I felt right now just wasn't the best. I signaled for the bartender to make me another drink.

As the night went on, Taylor and I had a good ass time. I was in the middle of the makeshift dance floor lost in the music. I felt a pair of hands wrap around my waist, and I continued to get lost in my steps. When I turned around, I was disappointed because it wasn't who I hoped for.

"Sup, Sherity?" the guy spoke, and I looked at him, trying to place his face because I didn't know who he was.

"Do I know you?"

"I'm a friend of your brother." He smirked. Knocking his hands off me.

"I don't have a brother," I replied and turned to walk off.

"That's fucked up you turned on your own family like that. You just be sure to tell Don that he better watch his back," he had the nerve to say.

I marched back to face him.

"You don't know shit about your so-called friend, or maybe you do, but you rape girls like he does. He got what he deserved, nasty bitch," I said and walked off. Grabbing Taylor by the hand, we stormed out the bar, and I started to hyperventilate.

"What was that all about?" Taylor asked. Shrugging my shoulders, I was ready for this night to be over with.

"He claims to be one of Rasheed's friends. Why don't nobody believe that he was a fucking rapist? Then what the hell does Don has to do with anything?" I sighed.

Taylor placed his arms around me to calm me down.

"I don't know, friend, but you need to let him know that at least for your own safety," Taylor suggested. Looking up at my friend, I nodded my head.

"I will, as a matter of fact, I'm about to handle this shit now, along with some other things." I sighed. I gave Taylor a peck on his cheek and then walked to my car after saying our goodbyes.

CHAPTER 11

DON

After Sherity left, I was somewhat pissed because I just needed time. Yeah, I had no reason to up and leave the way I did, but I just wasn't sure how she would take the truth either. I placed my focus on getting my money together and linking with Win business partner and opening my moving company Telhide Moving. It really did take up a lot of my time, but the things I was feeling for Sherity, I figured they would go away with her not being around me.

The slamming of a car door grabbed my attention, so I went to the window. Looking out, I saw Sherity making her way up the steps. She wasn't staggering and shit, so I assumed she wasn't drunk. Walking to the door, I opened it so that I could catch her before she walked into her condo. Sherity was standing there with her hand up like she was about to knock on my door.

"We need to fucking talk!" she spat and pushed her way inside. She's lucky that I wanted to talk to her to. Sherity tossed her purse on the couch and started to pace the floor.

"The fuck is your problem barging up in here like you run shit," I snapped.

"First of all, you're going to tell me what the fuck happened that night," she said neck rolling and shit and crossed her arms.

Her attitude was cute, but in no way was I moved by it. The

only reason why I was about to tell her the truth was because I had already decided I was and not because she came barging in asking.

"Man, sit your ass down!" I snapped. At first, I could tell she didn't want to, but she slowly took her seat, and I walked around and took mine beside her.

"Don't think you coming up in her running shit either. I'm telling you this because you have a right to know and that's it. After this is said, you can go on bout your business. You understand?"

Sherity rolled her eyes, but she nodded her head. Letting out a deep sigh, I grabbed the blunt from the ashtray and light that shit real quick. Taking the biggest toke, I held that shit in for a bit before blowing it out.

"Today would be nice," Sherity mumbled. I looked at her out the corner of my eye.

"While you being smart SheShe, I hope you'll be able to handle this shit I'm about to tell you. When I told you I was locked up, I been locked up since I was fifteen years old. I did twelve years for murder," I said, then stopped and looked at her.

Sherity's face still displayed attitude, so I wasn't sure if she had caught on right away.

"Sherity, I had a sister named Donna. Do you remember Donna?" I asked, lifting my brow. Sherity squinted her eyes, and they bucked a little.

"Do you remember my sister, Sherity?" I asked again through gritted teeth because I felt my emotions starting to come to head. She looked away, then started to shake her head.

"My sister was all I had until she got caught up with that nigga Rasheed. I don't know what kind of hold he had on her, but I wish she had never met that nigga. I killed your brother Sherity, and I'll do that shit again and again for the pain that he caused her. I saw my sister's body and how he left her. Every time I close my eyes, I see that shit." I barked and punched my fist.

"Did you know who I was?" she stuttered. When I looked back at her, she was crying.

"The fuck is you crying for and hell nah I ain't know who you were until gal brought that shit up at the wing spot. Talking about some it was weird for us to be together, so I asked her, and she was like she couldn't date the person who killed her brother. Then when you told me more of your story and all the shit that he did to you, that shit made me sick. Like I can't believe this nigga was really out here doing this shit to females. I bet you and my sister weren't the only ones either." I sighed.

Sherity scooted closer to me.

"Did you think that I was going to be mad or angry about who you were?"

"No, and honestly, I didn't care if you were." I shrugged.

"Thank you so much for saving me, and I'm forever grateful. I know what you did was for your sister, but you saved me as well. Oh my god!" Sherity gasped.

"What?'

"Shit, my main reason for coming over here was to tell you about this guy from the bar. While out with Taylor, we were dancing, and this guy approached me. He knew my name, but I didn't know who he was, said he was a friend of my brother, but I told him I didn't have a brother. Then he told me to tell you that you needed to watch your back. It caught me off guard, but now it makes sense." She frowned.

See, this was the type of shit I was talking about, dealing with me came with the bullshit. What if he just so happened wanted to send a message to me through Sherity but in a violent way? She ain't even have to tell me who the hell it was because I knew Toolie was behind all this shit. I found out that Toolie was Rasheed's half-brother.

"Did Rasheed have another brother, not by your moms?" I asked Sherity. Her entire demeanor changed, and I caught that shit.

"What Sherity don't fuck with me right now!" I snapped, causing her to jump.

"You don't know, do you?"

"Know what dammit!" I yelled, standing up.

"Teeaundre was there with Rasheed when he did that shit to your sister," she mumbled.

"How the fuck do you know?" I asked, grabbing her.

"Because when they got back to the house that night, I over-heard them talking about it, and they both changed from bloody clothes. Teeaundre just never got arrested for that he got locked up on some other shit," Sherity told me. I couldn't believe this shit. All this time, I could've been got at that nigga in the jam, and he knew all along who the fuck I was.

"I appreciate you telling me all this," I looked at Sherity, and she walked over to me, placing her hands on both sides of my face.

"I told you I was forever grateful for you, and I meant that," she leaned in and tried to place a kiss on my lips, and I moved my face.

"You got to go, SheShe. We can't do this," I sighed. Sex was the furthest thing on my mind, no matter what my dick was say-ing. Sherity dropped to her knees. While she was tugging at my gym shorts, I was trying to pull her up.

"Sherity me, and you can't be doing this no more," I strug-gled to say. My dick was sitting nicely in her hands, and she looked at me.

"Clearly, I'm not bothered by all this shit with my brother, but just let me enjoy myself one last time before we part ways," she said, then placed her entire mouth over my shit, making it disappear. I could do nothing but stare at the ceiling.

I continued to let SheShe do her thang until I was on the verge of nutting, and I picked her up and had her bent over on the couch. Sliding in my shit felt like it was at home after two months. Yeah, I knew I missed this pussy. Too bad this was about to be the last time I hit this shit.

It was something about this time that just felt different with Sherity. I would handle these niggas, and I would handle Toolie personally. In order to protect her, I was going to have to part ways from her.

Sherity threw herself into me as I continued to stroke her with deep thrusts. That last stroke almost took me out of here because I couldn't stand up afterwards. While I shot my kids inside of Sherity, I grabbed her and placed my head on her back so that I could catch my breath.

Once I had got myself together, I pulled out and headed to the bathroom to get Sherity a rag. When I heard the door slam, I knew then that she had left. I was hoping to at least clarify and leave off on a good page, but I'll just let it be since she already left. I pray what I told her didn't put any more on her because she needs nothing else messing with her mental.

CHAPTER 12
SHERITY

Staring at the computer screen, I kept letting the other night play in my head. I couldn't understand why Don was so easy to shut me out. I at least thought once we discussed everything and both of our truths came out that we would be good. I don't know why I wanted more with him, but I did. I found myself falling for this rude ass, complicated man. My heart went out to his sister and how I could see the pain in his eyes when he spoke about her. It was just something that could never be erased.

"Sherity, are you ready to head out?" Taylor poked his head in my office. I closed my laptop and nodded, yes.

I had initially given this case to Taylor to handle due to it being a bit much for me to take on, but the time was now that I be able to be another voice for an unheard little girl. Walking out of the office, we headed to our company car and climbed in.

"The police are already in the area in an unmarked car. We don't want to alarm them coming in," Taylor told me. I nodded my head but remained silent.

"You didn't have to do this, Sherity, or is something else bothering you. You've kind of been closed off since the other night," Taylor said. I could feel him looking at me.

"Taylor, I'm fine. This case isn't bothering me," I responded truthfully. Taylor sucked his teeth, and I knew he was aggravated.

"Taylor, I found out that Don is the one that murdered my brother," I let fly out my mouth. The car swerved, and Taylor slammed on breaks.

"What the fuck Taylor? Are you trying to kill us?" I screamed.

"I should be asking you that with that bomb you just dropped. Oh my god, spill it because I just know you all in your head," he said as he slowly pulled back off. During the remainder of the drive, I told him the entire story up until now. We pulled up to our destination.

"This is some Lifetime movie shit. So, what you gone do, just let him gone about his life? It's clear you have feelings for him," Taylor voiced.

"He needs time. I think he's got some other things on his plate, and I'm just not what he needs right now, no matter how bad I want him. I need to focus on getting myself together. You ready?"

"Yeah, come on," Taylor answered.

We both got out the car and walked up on the raggedy porch that looked like it was barely standing. I knocked on the door and waited for an answer. Taylor had already shifted to his work face just that quickly, and he wasn't about to play no games either.

"Yes," the woman came to the door and blew out a ton of smoke. Fanning the smoke out of my face, I showed her my ID.

"I'm Sherity Tyree from Social Services, and I wanted to take a look inside your home. It's part of the steps we have to take to see if your daughter will be able to return," I told her.

This bitch rolled her eyes and flicked the cigarette out the door. Moving to the side, I looked at her like she's lucky that shit didn't hit me. When she let us in, the place was shockingly cleaned and nice in décor. She took her seat as if she knew she was on her shit.

"Is there a Ronnie Jordan here?" Taylor asked.

"What you need Ronnie for?" she asked.

"Ma'am, are you aware of the allegations that had your child removed from your home?" I asked the lady.

"She wanted to be fast as hell and not follow the rules so ain't no telling what was told," the mother said. I shook my head in disbelief.

"So, you didn't even inquire to find out where she been all this time?" I asked.

"What's going on?" an older man walked into the living room, whom I assume was this Ronnie guy.

Taylor signaled for the police to enter.

"Ronnie Jordan, you're under arrest for the rape of a minor," I told him, but then I turned to the mother.

"Your daughter has been in your care, and for the longest, she has been victim to this molestation from your husband!" I spat.

"That girl is lying!" she shouted.

"We have enough DNA evidence to prove it as well as your daughter being pregnant by this man. I suggest you get y'all a good lawyer because she won't be back in this household period!" I spat.

Turning on my heels, I headed out the door. Even though she was shouting and cussing up a storm following us out of the house, I still had to hold my composure because I was on my job. This was the type of shit that made my blood boil, was the family members that allowed this shit to happen or turn a blind eye. It hurt me to my core, and I knew firsthand how this that girl felt. I lucked up and never got pregnant, but damn, what more evidence did she need?

Once in the car, I slammed the car door and waited on Taylor to wrap up everything. I wanted so bad to beat the fuck out of them folks. Looking out the window, I watched as Taylor headed to the car and got in.

"I swear sis I thought you were gone swing on that bitch. You did good." Taylor laughed, and so did I.

"On God, that hoe had it coming." I smiled.

"I swear I wouldn't want to work with anybody else." He smiled

"Let's have a seafood boil tonight at my house," I perked up.

"You know I'm down!" Taylor twerked in his seat.

◻ ◻ ◻

I had the music blasting and was blending up some Hennessey margaritas while Taylor was cutting up the sausages to go in our boil. I felt good for some reason, and nobody would bring me down.

"Taylor, you've been having a little too much fun with them sausages nigga. Don't forget we got to eat those," I joked.

Taylor looked at me and stuck his tongue out.

"Bitch, it's been so long since I had some these sausages starting to look real good over here," he replied, causing both of to bust out laughing.

I walked over and handed him his drink and started to sip from mine. Taking a seat on the couch, Usher "Confessions" came on the radio, and my mind went back to this guy that I used to date that had the nerve to pull this same shit on me. He was one of them relationships that I had just to say I had somebody.

A knock on the door pulled me from my thoughts and I just knew it wasn't Don because I didn't want to see him right now. Slowly, I walked over to the door and peeked through the peephole, and it was Loc. Loc turned out to be real cool.

Opening the door, he started laughing.

"Let me in," he whispered and slid in the door all fast.

"Are you not supposed to be over here?" I asked, starting to laugh at his antics.

"I told him I was leaving, but damn it seem like the party right here," he joked, heading to the kitchen where Taylor was still cooking.

"Aw yeah y'all doing it up over here," he said as he made his way back to the living room and took a seat in the chair across from me.

"So how may I help you, Loc? It seems you go back and tell Don everything I tell you." I sighed and lifted my brow.

"If that man knew I was over here about to say what I'm about to say, he would kill me. Look, I'm here because, for some odd reason, you done hit my nigga with the love bug or something."

"Loc, stop lying. I don't know what the hell this shit is we had going on, but I'm good and done with Don regardless of my feelings," I answered.

"So, you admit that you got feelings for him?" He leaned forward and looked at me.

"In a strange way, yes. I don't know what the hell his problem is," I mumbled.

"Not that it's an excuse but look at shit from his perspective. He doesn't know shit about no relationships or even how to love anyone properly not even himself. He went in at fifteen years old even then he was in the streets. You know what that nigga says every time I be like I love you bruh. He says some damn love don't love nobody. That's how he thinks.

When he lost his sister, his world crashed, so all these feelings that he's going through, he doesn't know how to handle that.

That man missed out on half of his life so I can see why he need to be taught some things. Honestly, my nigga needs some help because his issues are deeper than what's on the surface," Loc explained, and I instantly felt sorry for Don.

"So, what you want me to do chase him or some shit?"

"Not at all but just give him some time he will come around," Loc responded, and his phone rang,

"This that nigga now, Hello. Man damn you spying on a nigga. Aite," he laughed and hung up the phone.

"You been caught?" I asked.

"Yeah, nigga seen me walk over here. He got cameras, and I ain't even know that shit. That means he can see who comes and go over here too, that nigga ain't slick." Loc laughed and stood up to leave.

"Just remember what I said," he said before walking out the door.

Locking up the door, I leaned up against the door. Taylor rounded the corner and looked at me.

"I might as well start planning a wedding. I can see this shit now. Sis, once that man learns how to love wholeheartedly, you gone get the best version of his mean ass, and he probably won't ever love another the way he loves you," Taylor sighed and wiped away fake tears.

"Man, go head on with your dramatic ass," I shooed him away. No lies, if that were the case, I would welcome it.

CHAPTER 13

DON

After being on the road for a bit, I arrived at my destination, and I checked the cameras that I had installed outside of my place. When I saw Loc head over to the SheShe's house, I shook my head and wondered what he was up to. This nigga was on some other shit trying to play both sides between the two of us. Dialing his number, I waited on him to pick up.

"Hello!" he answered.

"I don't even care to hear the reason, but my cameras show that you at SheShe's house, get out," I said calmly.

"Damn, man, you spying on a nigga? Aite," he replied, and we hung up.

I placed my phone in the tray and kept my eyes on what I was looking for. When I saw the light cut off and on twice, I exited my car and walked up to the door. Once the door opened, I slid in and dapped it up with the warden.

"I see the street been treating you well," he spoke.

"Something like that," I answered dryly. Once we made it to his office, he turned to face me.

"Ok, listen. His cellmate is in the hole, so the fight that was started today worked out perfectly. He got the entire cell to himself. Put this on, and Officer J will escort you down to the corridor. Once y'all reach the corridor, the cameras will cut for approximately three minutes and forty-five seconds. Get in and get out," the warden spoke, giving me instructions. I grabbed the orange jumper that I surely didn't miss and headed to the bathroom to change.

"You just can't leave this alone, can you?" Donna asked.

I purposely tuned her out because this was getting done regardless. This entire time this nigga was in on Donna's death and walking around like ain't shit happen.

"You can ignore me all you want, but I also know that once you do this, it isn't going to change anything," she said.

Once I finished dressing, I looked at my sister and exited the bathroom.

"You ready?" he asked.

Nodding my head at the warden, Officer J walked in and escorted me out. Walking these corridors felt so natural after being here so long. It's crazy to say a nigga felt at home.

I made sure the knife in my hand was ready because it was go-time. As soon as we hit the corridor, Toolie cell was the first one there, and Officer J slowly moved the gate, letting me in. One inside, I walked over to the bed and placed my hand over his mouth, causing his eyes to pop open.

"This is for my sister, nigga," I told Toolie and ran the blade across his throat, tossing the pillow over his head. Just like that, I walked back out of the cell, and J closed the cell.

Letting out a deep breath, a smile eased on my face on the way back to the warden's office. That shit felt good as hell to do. It was like a nigga got off for killing him.

When I stepped back inside, I changed back into my street clothes and placed the knife in a bag that the warden gave me.

"I appreciate you letting me do this. When your shipment comes, it'll be a little extra in there, plus this," I said, handing him five grand.

"It's all good, anytime," he said, and we dapped each other up.

⬚ ⬚ ⬚

It was Sunday, and I decided to chill over my mom's house. She had the house smelling good while she got down in the kitchen, and I just sat there watching TV even though my mind was on Sherity. News traveled fast. Once everyone woke up and seen that Toolie had been killed, I already knew that they might think that I had something to do with it, but I didn't even care. My crew was already on them other nigga's neck that was walking around here, sending messages and shit. They weren't going to be breathing for too much longer.

"Did you tell Loc I was cooking today?" my mom hollered from the kitchen.

"Yeah!" I yelled back. My cell went off. Looking at the screen, I saw it was Win.

"Hello."

"Mi nuh undastand wah gwaan?" Win said in his thick accent. I ain't know what the hell he said.

"Aye, I don't understand all that." I sighed.

"Mi don't understand what's going on. News travels fast. Did you order the hit on Toolie?"

"I ain't order shit. I did it myself because I found out he was there when that shit went down with my sister. That's why that nigga had beef with me all this time and putting his boys on me," I revealed.

"Mi see now. Are you done?"

"Not quite, but I'm gone chill for a bit."

"You might be in the wrong profession." He laughed.

"Nah, but I want these motherfuckers to know that I'm not to be fucked with, and I don't care about shit, so it's nothing to knock a bitch off." I shrugged.

"You can have men to handle all that for you and still send the same message. I'm very much powerful, but my days of doing dirty work are over. Learn the teachings that I'm trying to give you. You now have things to lose, so it's a must you move differently. Just say the word, and it's handled."

I respected Win for trying to school me.

"I want that entire crew handled when they least expect it," I told Win.

"Done. Enjoy your day," he said and disconnected the call.

As soon as I hung up, my mom walked into the living room, wiping her hands off on her apron and took a seat. I could feel her gaze on me, so I looked at her.

"What?" I asked. My mother smiled, showcasing her pearly whites and open-faced gold tooth.

"I'm proud of you for opening the moving company," she said. I shrugged my shoulders.

"That ain't nothing," I sighed and faced back to the TV.

"Yes, the fuck it is, DonMir! Why do you always downplay yourself like you can do nothing great? Like it ain't a big deal. For somebody to be free, you're always just down!" she snapped.

"You got something that is yours, that belongs to you. On top of that, you don't have to stop there. You can open up so many more companies in different states and cities. This what I was trying to get you to see. You twenty-seven years old, and I might not agree with what you do, but eventually, you can sit back and enjoy the fruits of your labor and let that drug shit go. Motherfuckers don't sell drugs to make it a lifelong commitment. Hell, they invest that shit and more profits. You might think I'm constantly bitching at you, but that's my job. You all I got now," she sighed. I wasn't angry at my mom because she was making sense.

"I'm fucked up, man. Donna really fucked me up in the head. I swear no matter how hard I try to forget that shit, it's there, and it turned me into this person who I just don't know. I know nothing else but to be this hard ass nigga that don't mind dying behind my respect or name. A nigga don't want to be like this," I admitted.

My ma got up and came to sit down beside me.

"Listen to me. I don't want you to think I hate you for what you did. I was just hurting because I lost you too. Donna is in a place far better than here on earth. I always just look at it like, when it's my time, I'll be happy to be with my baby again. That's why I don't walk around depressed or mad at the world. When I get lonely, I talk to her let her know how I feel because sometimes I just feel her there." She sighed.

"I see her. She comes to visit me so much that I can't get rid of her when I want to. She has my back even when she not here physically," I finally told her.

"Wow, it seems to me she hasn't crossed over because somebody won't let her go or either her job isn't done," my mom smiled.

"I met this girl, and I think, well, I know I feel something for her. It's just a nigga don't feel like I'm good enough for her because I don't know how to love anybody."

"You don't know how to love anybody, Don? You've loved only Donna and me in your lifetime. Who is this girl?" she asked. I wasn't sure how she was going to take this, but I felt she would understand once I told her everything.

"Her name is Sherity. She lives across the hall from me, but this is the crazy part," I said and filled my mom in on everything about Sherity leaving nothing out.

"Oh my god, my heart goes out to that girl. That's a lot to take in a deal with. So, does she seem to be bothered with who you are?"

"Not at all, she said she would forever be grateful because I saved her. I can tell she's got some type of feelings for me, but I ain't gone lie. I just be pushing shorty off," I said.

"Whatever this may be that takes place between the two of y'all can work or it can be a disaster if y'all don't get the help you both need. I say that to say this, you have never loved anyone outside of your sister and me, so you have to love her differently. She is fragile, and you are fragile too. You might be a man, but you fucked up as well. Both of y'all are coming to each other with different types of pain. Yes, you can move from it, but it might be damaging if you don't take the time to work on yourself. You might not know how to love a woman properly because you haven't been shown that or given that. She might be the one to love you if you let her. It will come naturally, and for her, she has this thing with the male species far as trust, but it seems to me that you are different," my ma smiled and grabbed my hand.

"Her drinking problem though, it's just crazy how she can switch up from day and night."

"That's why she needs to get some help. You might be the one she needs to redirect her from that bottle. Look, I'm not gone tell you anything wrong, but you deserve to be happy. It's time. Just don't give up on something that you never quite had." My mom stood up and kissed my forehead and headed back to the kitchen.

◻ ◻ ◻

After dinner with mama, I walked out on the porch and took a seat. I hated this neighborhood and couldn't understand why mama wouldn't let me get her up out of here. Looking out on how much it changed over the years was a story within itself. The night I got arrested popped in my head, and how my mother's face was etched in hurt will never be erased. I heard the door swing open, and it was mama handing me the food she had packed up for me.

"Thanks, mama," I said, getting up to grab the food.

"I put some extra in there, so maybe you and Sherity can have that talk over my peach cobbler," she smiled. I leaned down and kissed her on the cheek.

"Ion know about that sharing your peach cobbler is kind of hard," I joked. Mama slapped me on the arm.

"Boy, you bet not. Everything will work out, son," she reassured me and went back inside the house.

CHAPTER 14

SHERITY

While the music blasted in the background, I continued to scrub the baseboards in the hallway. My mind was in overdrive, so I was taking it out on cleaning solutions and the baseboards in order for me not to pick up a drink. I hummed along to the sounds of DVSN.

"Don't be sorry just be careful baby know my heart is fragile," I sang with so much passion.

There was a small knock at the door, and I just looked at the door because I knew Taylor was spending the day with his boo, so it couldn't be him. It could only be one person, and I wasn't sure if I wanted to continue facing him. Tossing the brush back into the bucket, I got up and walked to the door. When I opened the door, Don stood there looking so fucking decadent holding a bag. He held it up.

"Peace offering, plus my moms told me to feed you." He cracked a smile but let it quickly fade. I moved over to let him in and locked the door back.

"Look, Don, I don't have the energy to deal with whatever it is if it's negative. I am drained," I admitted.

"Just sit down and eat," he spoke. He didn't even bother to look at me. He was so fucking distant at times.

I plopped my ass down on the couch and waited on him to

hand me my plate. The smell of the home cooked meal made my stomach growl. Immediately I picked up the pieces of cornbread that were sitting on the plate and took a bit. Closing my eyes, I savored the flavor.

"She sent you some peach cobbler too, but you're not getting that until we talk." He smirked.

I shrugged my shoulders and continue to find myself in the plate that I was holding. Don just watched me eat. I assumed he had eaten already because he touched nothing the entire time I ate.

"So, what's up?" I asked, placing the plate on the table. Don ran his hands over his waves and faced me.

"You know all this shit is new to me as far as expressing my feelings and shit. I do know that I feel something for you, and even though I have never been in a relationship, I want to try that with you. A nigga is flawed as hell, and you know I deal with a lot of shit, but I have room for you to show me how to love you. If you're willing to do the same," he said.

My mouth hung open in shock because I couldn't believe this even came out of his mouth. I placed my hand on his head to see if this nigga was sick.

"Man, go head on with that shit. I'm serious," he said, knocking my hand off his head.

"I mean, why the sudden change?"

"Does it matter? Are you willing to ride it out with me?" he asked. I sat quietly thinking about what he said. I wanted to scream, yes, and this was the only way that I could move forward and heal.

"What if this doesn't work with us? We both have so many things to heal from."

"That's why we don't have to rush into this. We can take it a day at a time, but I want us to both go to therapy and some type of counseling. I think not only do we need private sessions to work on our personal issues, but we need to go together as well so that we can work as one," Don said.

"Well, I guess the only thing to do is eat that peach cobbler then," I smiled, letting him know that I was willing to take this journey with him.

"I guess you can have this shit, then shorty." He laughed and handed me the bowl with the cobbler in it.

"So, shit you got the place smelling like straight bleach, did I interrupt your cleaning?" Don leaned back to get comfortable.

"I'm trying to stop drinking, so instead of fixing me a drink, I turned to a new alternative," I admitted.

"Yeah, I'm gone need for you lay off the oil. We're gone slowly get through this so that the drinking shit can cease," he mumbled. I climbed on top of his lap and looked at Don in his dark eyes.

"Don't think the worst of this," I whispered and placed my lips on his.

For the remainder of the night, I did my best to please him and showed him the difference of being intimate with someone you care about instead of the usual sex we had, which wasn't bad, but it was time for something different. I even showed him how to please me the correct way.

〇 〇 〇

The next morning, I rolled over, and to my surprise, Don was gone. I had to be out of it not to notice him leave. Looking around, I felt some type of way because I thought things went well last night. Tossing the covers back, I slid out of bed and went to the bathroom to handle my hygiene so that I could get ready for work. Turning on the light, I noticed a note on the sink.

I had to make some moves shorty, be good today.

I smiled at his gesture even though, at first, I felt some type of way. That put a pep in my step and had me moving gracefully while I did all I had to do this morning. Once I was dressed, I headed out.

As soon as I stepped outside, the gloomy skies kind of dampen my spirit. Not letting it get to me, I hit the lock on my car and hopped in.

Kelly Price "It's Gonna Rain" came blaring through the speakers, and I started to sing along to the lyrics. I had that song on repeat my entire drive to work. When I pulled up at work, my phone started to ring. Don's name popped up on the screen, which was weird. It hit me that we had never exchanged numbers.

"Hello," I answered all smiles.

"I realized this morning that you and I never swapped numbers. Now that I got to keep tabs on you and shit, I called my phone this morning from your phone and saved it," he said in his usual deep tone.

"Hmm, that's all good, but I'm just wondering exactly how you got in my phone?" I asked.

"A nigga dicked you into a coma, but it was nothing your fingerprint couldn't do," he replied.

"I got to watch you and your sneakiness," I whispered.

"I just wanted to tell you to have a good day, SheShe."

"Thank you, Don. You do the same." I sighed, and we disconnected the call.

Grabbing my bag, I got out of the car and walked toward the building.

"Sherity!" my name was called from behind me. Turning on my heels, I looked in the direction it came from. As the girl drew near, I froze even though I wanted to take off.

"Shameese," I mumbled.

Shameese and I used to be connected at the hip. She was my first cousin but more like my best friend back when we were kids. Just like everyone else, she was a part of the life that I left alone.

"Hey, Sherity," she said, catching her breath.

"What do you want? It's been a very long time," I asked, shifting my weight to one leg.

"I know, and I apologize for that, but it's granny. She's not doing well, and she wants to see you," she had the nerve to say.

Out of everyone in my family, I missed my granny the most. It shocked me the day that she just up and abandoned me like the rest. I didn't even have a response. Shameese stepped closer to me, and she placed her hand on my wrist, causing me to jerk away.

"Cousin, I should've been reached out to you after everything went down, but I had my own demons to deal with. You know Teeaundre is dead," she mentioned, not that I gave a damn.

"What does that have to do with me? The one person that I expected to have as some type of support just up and left. You knew the shit that he did to me and could've backed me up when everyone turned on me!" I snapped.

"Sherity, he tried me too with Teeaundre. I was so embarrassed because at your graduation party I had my own secrets to deal with. He forced me to do some things I wasn't proud of. I end up doing it, and then I started messing with Teeaundre to the point that I was pregnant at your party. Girl, when you left and went to college, I left the city and started over someplace else.

I eventually told granny because you came up in conversation when I was telling her about Toolie. I hated both of them niggas, but even behind bars, he took care of our daughter," she said, leaving me standing there with shock all over my face.

I couldn't believe all this shit. What the hell was wrong with my brother? It was like he hurt every female he encountered.

"Look, I have to get to work, tell granny I'll stop by later," I told her, leaving her standing there.

I hurried into the building. This was not how I needed to start my day. I swear if it wasn't one thing, it was another. Coming down the hall, I headed to Taylor's office and walked inside. Only to see that he wasn't there. Shit, I needed to talk, and his ass ain't even here. Heading to my office, I pulled my phone out and called his phone. His phone went straight to voicemail.

"Taylor, bitch, why the hell you ain't at work? I got some tea," I said and hung up the phone.

◻ ◻ ◻ ◻

Hours had passed, and Taylor still ain't make it into work or returned my call. It was now lunchtime, so I was going to run by his house to see if he was at home. He was probably somewhere in a dick coma like I was this morning. I continued to call his phone as it kept going to voicemail. At this point, I was getting annoyed, whipping into the spot next to Taylor's car put a little ease on me. Reaching into the glove compartment, I pulled out the extra set of keys that we kept for each other places in case of emergencies.

Taylor lived in some nice townhomes about fifteen minutes away from our job downtown. I used the key to let myself in, and the sight before me instantly sent me in a panic. Taylor's living room was trashed. His flat screen was knocked over, and shit was thrown everywhere.

"Taylor!" I yelled and made my way through the rest of downstairs.

Suddenly, I hit the steps and headed upstairs. When I entered Taylor's bedroom, I let out a gut-wrenching scream. Running over to Taylor's body, I almost threw up at the scene before me. Dropping to my knees, I cried uncontrollably while I dialed 911.

CHAPTER 15

DON

Loc and I had just wrapped up a meeting with Win and was still hanging around at his crib. His wife Kyelle had made some lunch, so we were just kicked back chilling. I looked off into the pool, and a slight smile formed on my face when I thought about SheShe.

"Nigga, you've been over there cheesing and shit and looking spaced out what you got going on," Loc asked.

"Mi not want to say noting, but I saw that too," Win added.

"Aite after talking with moms yesterday, she put some shit in my head, and SheShe and I decided to give this shit a try." I smiled.

Loc shoved me a bit.

"I told your ass you were feeling shorty. I was rooting for y'all anyway. SheShe seems like she's good people, no matter her past," Loc mentioned.

My phone vibrated on the table and picked it up. It was a picture message from an unknown number, so I clicked on the message.

"The fuck is this shit?" I barked and tossed the phone to Loc and Win.

"Ain't that your girl's homeboy Taylor or some shit?" Loc

asked, looking at me. I nodded my head and hung my head down. This was some fucked up shit.

Win slide me back the phone and looked at me.

"You still want to wait until things die down. They sending messages loud and clear," He stood up. I looked at him, and if I knew anything, I knew this had Toolie's crew name all over it and was sending a message because of Toolie's death.

"For Toolie" was the message they sent with the picture.

"Them niggas got to go ASAP! Do whatever," I looked at Win. I hopped up and grabbed my stuff.

"I got to go find SheShe!" I snapped. I tried calling her phone, but she wasn't answering.

"I'm rolling with you just in case them niggas roll up!" Loc spat.

As soon as we got in the car, I dialed SheShe back, hoping that she answered the damn phone. Finally, after the fifth damn time, she answered, and I could barely make out what she was saying due to her crying.

"Where you at SheShe?" I asked, talking over her.

"I'm at Taylor's," she sobbed.

"Baby, what's the address. I'm heading to you now." Sherity called off the address, and Loc put it in his phone.

"I'm on the way. Do not leave!" I spat and hung up the phone.

"Fuck!" I yelled and hit the steering wheel. These niggas needed to be handled, and I meant ASAP. Why the hell did they have to do that boy like that?

"SheShe just can't catch a break," Loc said and shook his head.

☐ ☐ ☐

I finally made it to Sherity, and the police was everywhere.

I placed the strap I had underneath the seat before getting out of the car. Sherity was sitting on the hood of her car just staring off into space.

"SheShe," I called out, and she looked over at me and slid off the car to run in my arms. Once her face hit my chest, she just broke down again.

"How can someone do this to him? He didn't bother no one or nothing. I gave them the name of the guy he had been seeing because he said he was with him yesterday," Sherity sobbed.

All I could do was shake my head because I knew the truth, and whoever dude was had nothing to do with this.

"Taylor neighbor's had cameras so they gave the footage to the police hoping they can catch something," she told me.

All I did was continue to stroke her back because I couldn't tell her what I wanted to tell her while we were out here.

"Ms. Tyree," an officer walked up to Sherity and me.

"Yes," she answered while wiping her face.

"I just wanted to keep you up to date. Now we watched the camera footage from the neighbor's camera and I just want to show you this. If you look here a little before midnight, you see the guy who you told us was Bryant leave in his car. At approximately 1:15 a.m., you see someone walk up to the door. The body type differs from that of Bryant. Whoever this was, was in the house for eleven minutes, then you see them running away from the house. Bryant said he left because he had to return to work, and once we called his job, they were able to provide us with info that Bryant was there and indeed on the clock until ten o'clock this morning. Are you sure that your friend didn't have any other friends or any enemies?" he asked Sherity. I could tell she was getting frustrated.

"I'm positive," she mumbled.

"Here's my card, if you hear anything else or need anything

give me a call," he told her. Sherity grabbed the card, and the officer walked off.

"Do you think you good enough to drive, or do you want to leave your car here?" I asked.

"I can drive," she mumbled, and I walked her to her car.

"I will be right behind you," I told her and kissed her on the lips. Helping her in the car, I closed the door and walked back to my truck, where Loc was waiting.

"She good?" he asked.

"Hell nah, and now I got to tell her the truth because after the footage, it shows it couldn't be of the person who she thought done it since he's got an alibi. She not gone feel right until she gets some answers about Taylor." I sighed and pulled behind Sherity to trail her.

"Ion know bruh. This one is different. She might not take it as easy as she did her brother. Her brother deserved to die, but Taylor was her fucking right hand. She's gone be mad than a motherfucker when she finds out this got your name all on it," Loc said, telling me what I didn't want to hear.

"I know, but I can't lie to her. That ain't in me, and the last thing I need is to start lying when we trying to be together!" I spat.

"Shit, that's even if she wants your ass now once you tell her this shit. Nigga, Taylor was to her like we are to each other."

All I did was nod my head, but I had made my mind up. There was no way that I could lie to her. I turned the music up to tune out the truth and trailed Sherity all the way home.

Once we got to the condo, Loc went to my place, and I helped Sherity inside of hers. My girl looked terrible, and it was nothing I could do to take away her pain. She just stood there in the middle of the floor, looking around. Finally, she walked over to the table and picked up a picture of her and Taylor.

"It's just way too many memories here," she whispered and looked at me. "Can I stay at your place for a few days?"

"You know you can," I told her. Sherity headed to the bedroom to pack her a bag, I guess, so I followed her back there.

"I just don't know who would do something like this, like that shit keeps playing in my head," she cried.

"Sherity, we need to talk," I started, and she held her hand up and shook her head.

"I don't want to hear shit right now because I just know it's some bullshit to follow!" she spat. I walked over to her and sat her down on the bed.

"You got to listen to me. As bad as I don't want to tell you this shit, I can't lie to you."

"I just lost my fucking friend I don't have time to deal with whatever lies you bout to tell," she spat.

"Sherity shut up and listen to me, please. I know who is behind Taylor's murder, and they will be taken care of," I quickly blurted out before she could interrupt me.

"The hell you just say?"

"Look, I don't know if it done got back to you or not yet, but Toolie's dead. I did that shit once you told me that he was with Rasheed. Toolie has been having a hit on me ever since I got out. Once word got out that Toolie was dead, his niggas must've been looking at a way to get back at me by hurting your boy." I sighed.

Sherity started swinging on a nigga, and I reached out and grabbed her arms.

"Stop fucking hitting me!" I yelled.

"This is all your fault. Why the hell do you keep killing people? If you had of just left that shit alone, my friend would still be alive!" she yelled.

"Do you not understand these niggas are out to hurt anything connected to me? You were a fucking target too. That nigga that sent you that warning knew you and guess what probably been following y'all asses because they knew where Taylor laid his head. You're not exempt from this. I just handled shit that needed to be handled!" I spat.

"Get out! I don't even want to look at you, Don," Sherity cried. I didn't move. Sherity smacked me so hard I almost forgot who she was.

"Gooooo!" she yelled.

"I'm gone go, but you need to know that you ain't safe out here. Do know that the nigga that killed Taylor will be handled. I'll do all that shit again for anybody that ever hurt you, SheShe," I told her before walking out of her room.

As I walked down the hall, Sherity's cries did something to me. I knew she didn't need to be left alone, but I also knew she wasn't gone let me stay. I walked out of the door and into my condo. Loc was sitting on the couch already had the blunt lit and passed it to me.

"How it go?" he asked. I took a hit of the blunt and blew the smoke out.

"Not good, she's pissed at a nigga. She smacked my ass and tried to fight me. I had to remember she was hurting because I almost forgot who she was," I sighed. Loc shook his head.

"Just give her some time. She'll come around," he said. I didn't know about that, but I sure hope like hell she did.

CHAPTER 16
SHERITY

A Week Later

My phone had been ringing off the hook, and it woke me from my drunken slumber. Grabbing the phone, I answered without even looking.

"Hello," I answered groggily.

"Sherity, it's Shameese," they replied.

I pulled the phone back and looked at the phone because I knew she didn't have my number. That's when I realized she had called me through Facebook. I have to remember after this funeral to make my damn page back private.

"What is it, Shameese?" I asked as I sat up in the bed.

"Well, you never showed up that day to see granny, and I heard about your friend Taylor, so first, I want to offer my condolences."

"Thanks, I didn't make it because he died that day. I'll come by today."

"Ok, see you later," Shameese said. I hung up the phone.

Today was about to be the longest day, and I don't know why I said I would come by today knowing I had to go view Tay-

lor's body. His funeral was tomorrow, and I just wasn't prepared
to say goodbye or even see him like this. His mother tried so hard
to get me to take part in the planning of his funeral, but I just
couldn't do it. I hadn't even left the house for work, the first few
days I attempted to work from home, but I had to use the vac-
ation days I had built up to grieve.

Pulling myself from the bed, I stepped over the trash and
clothing that I had on the floor. Once I got to the bathroom, I
turned the shower on. Staring in the mirror, I looked a damn mess.
My once shiny skin was dull and ashy looking. My hair hadn't been
combed in days. I pulled my hair out of the ponytail so I could
wash it.

Stepping in the shower, I let the water cascade over my
head and body.

"Now you know you need to get yourself together bitch," Taylor
said. I kept my eyes closed because I had been hearing him a lot
lately.

*"I'm not playing with you, Sherity. You have disappointment
letting yourself go like this. Your one damn drink away from AA and
you, this is ridiculous. Make me come back and whoop your ass,"* he
said.

My eyes opened, and I saw the prettiest version of Taylor.
Even though you couldn't tell because my face was wet, I was
crying.

"I miss you, Taylor. What am I supposed to do without
you?" I asked.

*"Wheww, chile, I don't know because you didn't listen to me
when I was alive, so I might not have much pull dead either,"* he
smacked and rolled his eyes.

"Still dramatic in the afterlife?"

*"Always boo. Look, although you were so close, I could feel it.
You were about to reach that peak of happiness, so don't give up now.*

I'm going to be fine, and the Lord might kick me out after this, but I'm gone be even better when Don gets those niggas responsible. I'm handing him my torch to take care of you and look out for you. He will be so much better than me. I love you, Sherity, and I want you to be happy. Clean this nasty ass house once you finish washing your ass," he laughed.

Taylor was gone just like that. After a few more washes and washing my hair, I wrapped up and got out the shower. Looking at my house, I didn't have the time to clean, but maybe I'll get to it later. Once I got dressed, I brushed my hair up in a high bun and threw on the biggest pair of shades I could find and headed out the door.

I flew down the steps and to my car in hopes of not running into Don. I had been ignoring him for the last week and didn't plan on speaking to him. Every day he would call or send a text. Yes, I would read them, but I never responded. He was still so apologetic and letting me know that he was here for me if I needed anything. The thing was I wanted nothing he had to offer.

Reaching into my purse, I pulled out a miniature shot bottle of Vodka and tossed it back. I decided I would go see my granny first, and I needed to take the edge off.

It had been so long since I'd been to my granny's house due to the fact, I would simply avoid the neighborhood just like I did my parents' house. I remember so vividly running down these very sidewalks with Shameese and hanging out on the porch with granny sipping tea. The memories made me tear up a little.

I pulled in the driveway and cut the engine. Biting down on my bottom lip, I wasn't sure why my granny wanted to see me after all these years, but I was ready to get this over with. Sliding out the car, I adjusted my shades on my face and walked up to the door. As soon as I stepped on the porch, the door opened, and Shameese stood there with a smile on her face. The little girl that stood beside her looked like a younger version of her thank god she didn't look like Toolie. Thinking about Toolie and Don's admission started to make me feel weird, looking at his child.

"I didn't think you were coming this early." Shameese smiled and let me in.

"Sherity, please, before you go back there to see granny, I want to warn you. She has been sick for a little minute, so she might not look the same to you. Also, I really want us to work on our relationship. I miss you," she cried. Could I really have a relationship with her after all this time? The trust and everything would have to be restored.

"I'm dealing with a lot right now, and it's a bit much, but I could really use somebody to help me through this battle before I lose my shit," I admitted and was shocked that I even allowed it to come out of my mouth.

"I got you, cuz." She smiled and reached in to hug me.

As I looked around, nothing much had changed inside my grandmother's house. She even still had pictures of me around. Walking down the hallway to her room, I just looked at the trail of photos on the wall remembering the happier times. Stopping right at her bedroom door, I tried to mentally prepare myself for what I was about to see. Taking a deep breath, I entered her bedroom, which had been turned to a makeshift hospital room.

"She didn't want to go to hospice. She said she wanted to die peacefully in her home," Shameese whispered.

Looking at the bed, my granny was so small. She was a nice size woman because we often called her big mama. To see that she was half the size she was to where the bed was literally swallowing her just broke me down.

Shameese grabbed me to keep me from falling on the floor.

"She is okay. Go over there and talk to her," she told me as she held me and slowly walked over to the bedside with me.

"Granny!" I whispered, and she slowly opened her eyes. It was like she cracked a slight smile when she saw me.

"Sherity," she mumbled.

"Yes, it's me, granny," I removed my shades so that she could get a clear view of my face. Shameese hit a button on the bed, and the top of it lifted her a little bit so that she could see my face.

"Lord baby, I'm so glad Sha was able to find you," she spoke.

"Why after all these years, granny? The one person that I thought would never leave me did, and that hurt me to the core," I voiced. I had to know.

"When you left, I battled with what you said. That was until Shameese told me that it was the truth, and he had tried her as well. I went to your mother and spoke her out so badly because I was angry that she didn't believe it. You were already gone and changed your number, so I had no way of getting in contact with you because my own child turned on me, and I stopped coming around. Your mother has gone off the deep end, and I don't know where I went wrong with that child," she softly spoke and stopped to catch her breath.

"Thank God for Shameese coming back. That was the only way I could find you. You know I know nothing about no internet. I prayed many nights that God would send you back in its own way, so I stayed hopeful."

I bent down and laid on my granny, hugging her.

"I'm so sorry for not believing you about the sick ways of your brother. I hope he didn't damage you too badly. I know how that goes," she sighed. Looking up at her, I was saddened at her news.

"You know what it feels like?" I asked. She nodded her head, and I just left it at that.

"I just want you and Shameese to know that I have everything done up for y'all to split everything down the middle. When Willie Earl died that automatically left Shameese with his half, and since your mother ain't talking to me, she ain't getting shit of mine," my granny spoke. I couldn't help but chuckle a little. Willie Earl was her only son.

"Granny, I can't stay long because I have to go view my friend's body. I will come back, though." Granny patted my hand, letting me know that it was fine.

Before leaving the house, I turned to Shameese and gave her an enormous hug.

"Here put my number in your phone," I told her, holding my hand out. Shameese gave me her phone, and I entered my number.

"Call me whenever," I told her.

◻ ◻ ◻

When I left my granny's house, I felt lighter. I don't know why but the conversation that was held lifted some things from my spirit.

I just couldn't bring myself to my next destination, so. I drove extra slow to the funeral home, taking the longest route possible. Reaching into my bag, I pulled two of the miniature shots of Vodka I had left out and tossed them back. Popping a piece of mint gum in my mouth to mask the alcohol smell, I tried to get myself together. I didn't do drugs, but I so desperately needed something because the alcohol wasn't numbing me enough.

I sat outside the funeral home and watched the many people walk in and out. Damn, I should've asked Shameese to come with me because I couldn't do this by myself. A knock on the window startled the fuck out of me, and I jumped so damn hard. When I looked up, it was Don. I rolled my eyes and looked straight ahead. What the fuck was he doing here?

"He's here to be the support system you need, bitch, so let that man love you correctly. I think he is doing a good job for someone that doesn't know how to love," Taylor said popping up again.

"You've always been team Don, so that's easy for you to

say." I sighed.

"Who the hell are you talking too?" I could hear Don through the glass. I opened the door and got out, standing there looking at him. He was dressed in all black and smelled so fucking good.

"What are you doing here?" I asked, locking my doors.

"You really want to do this alone? I figured you need somebody." He shrugged. As if Taylor knew what he would say. Don leaned toward me, and I quickly turned my head.

"Have you been drinking, SheShe?" he frowned.

"Are you gone walk me in or be my daddy?" I snapped and started to walk toward the funeral home. I was walking so fast that he was a few steps behind me.

Once I entered the funeral home, it was like my legs shut down. They grew heavy and wouldn't move any further. Once you stepped inside the place, Taylor's body was the first room there, so I didn't have to walk far. I felt a hand in the small of my back.

"I'm right here, you got it," Don whispered.

It was like my hand had a mind of his own, and it reached and grabbed Don's hand. I knew I probably was squeezing the hell out of his hand, but oh well. I took one step, and it felt like Don carried me the rest of the way because I don't even remember walking before I knew it, I was next up to view the casket. Taylor looked so peaceful in his pink suit. I smiled at the fact that his mother honored his requests. For so long when he came out to her, she struggled to accept it, but she eventually came around. Inching slowly to the casket, I caressed his cold face.

"Girl, these folks got me looking dead. Mama could've hired a bitch a decent MUA," Taylor smacked. I tried to hide my laugh because this wasn't the time for it.

"Shut up!" I said as I leaned closer and placed a kiss on his face.

"I'm not even gone ask who you're talking too," Don mumbled and stepped back to give me a little space. I just stood there for the longest. I didn't want to leave him at all.

Finally, I was able to remove myself and register within my brain that my friend was at peace. I was still saddened because it wasn't fair that he was taken away from me suddenly, and I didn't even get to say goodbye. Don and I walked outside, and he walked me to my car. Turning to him, I opened my mouth to speak, but he beat me to it.

"I'm sorry for bringing you this pain," he blurted out.

"I'm sorry, too, for being so angry with you for what you did. I mean, I'm still fucked up that my friend is gone, but he is adamant about you for some reason," I smiled.

"Is that who you've been talking to looking like a crazy person?" Don asked, shocking me. I nodded my head.

"I swear Donna be doing the same shit. Shit be irking at times, but to know that she right there with me along the way, it kind of makes me feel good," he told me.

"Yeah, it does because Taylor didn't have a filter here on earth, and it's obvious, he doesn't have one in the afterlife either," I smiled. Don reached over and removed my shades to look at me in my eyes.

"When I met you, you used to have this glow about you, and I hate that it isn't there anymore," he told me.

"I gave up on myself," I admitted.

"Well, we're gone help you find her again. We were headed in the right direction, and I don't want us to go backwards," Don closed the space between us and lifted my face to his.

"I'm not going anywhere, SheShe. I got you," he whispered.

"Are you sure somebody else ain't been teaching you the

things I'm supposed to be teaching you?" I asked.

"I don't know where this shit is coming from, but I was told it comes naturally," he said, backing up and removing his ringing phone from his pocket.

"Yeah, boss," he answered. Don looked at me, and a smirk was on his face.

"Aite bet," he said and pushed some more buttons on his phone.

"I need to show you something. It might not be a pretty sight though," he looked at me and said.

"What is it?" I asked. Loc turned the phone around and showed me the pictures, and I quickly turned my head.

"Oh my god," I almost threw up.

"Those niggas been handled, and that's for Taylor," he winked. Don't ask me what came over me, but I wanted Don in the worse way.

"I really want you in the worst way right now, but I have stop back by my granny's place," I told him.

"Your granny? I thought you ain't have no family."

"Yeah, my cousin found me and told me that my granny was sick and wanted to see me. I went to go see her today, and I forgive her and my cousin. My grandmother was disowned by her own child because she started to believe me after she found out about my cousin. Rasheed and both Toolie tried her, and that resulted in her having a daughter by him," I told Don.

"This shit is wild, though. How does she feel about the Toolie situation?" I knew why he was asking since he was responsible for his murder.

"She's fine. All she has is his daughter, and she said that he was taking care of her, but she feels the same about him as I did Rasheed. I want you to meet them. Follow me over there," I suggested.

"Let's roll then. SheShe, for future references, the things that I do to protect you or my loved ones, aren't for everyone to know. I realize that's your cousin, but she doesn't need to know details," he called out.

"Most definitely," I replied and got in the car.

Pulling out of the funeral home, I stopped at the red light and looked in the rearview to see Don pulling up behind me. Things were looking up, and now all I wanted to do was bury my friend, clean my house, and get back to work. I wanted to take back over my life. It was like even though I had been through nothing but turmoil lately and was at my lowest that something was pushing me to be back on top. My grandmother coming back into my life was bittersweet because there wasn't telling how much time I had left with her.

My phone started ringing, and I answered.

"Hello."

"Sherity, it's Shameese. Granny is on the way to the hospital. After you left, she started coughing up blood," she cried.

"Ok, what hospital I'm on the way I was actually heading back to y'all right now?"

"We on the way to Saint Thomas," she cried. I disconnected the call, and when the light turned green, I drove off.

BOOM!

CHAPTER 17

DON

I took it upon myself to wait for Sherity outside of the funeral home today, hoping that she showed up. Since the night that Taylor died, she wasn't fucking with a nigga at all. No matter how hard I tried, she wasn't going. It made me feel good when she took me up on my offer to accompany her inside the funeral home. I knew she would be struggling through this.

Accepting her being mad at me, I understood to the fullest, and I would still do that shit again. It's crazy how I meet this girl, and both our lives end up connecting in the strangest ways. When I first pulled up on her, I was disappointed to smell the liquor on her, and that was my number one goal not to let her dig herself into a deeper hole.

I sat behind her at the light and had Loc on the phone, letting him know how shit went down.

"Man, see, look how all this shit worked out. Did you tell her about our other company you're opening in Memphis?"

"Nah, my focus is her right now. That company will be there. I'm just focused on her needs," I admitted.

"Is this DonMir motherfucking Telhide speaking? The nigga that claims love don't love nobody. This nigga done got soft." He laughed.

All I could do was laugh. The light changed, and Sherity

pulled off. As soon as I put my foot on the gas, another car coming from the other direction hit her so hard that the entire vehicle flipped over.

"Fuck! No!" I yelled.

"The fuck going on, bruh?" Loc was yelling, but I had already hopped out of the car and ran full speed to her car.

"Somebody call the police!" I yelled. I started to smell gas and tried my best to get Sherity door open so that I could pull her from the car, but she was pinned.

"Don't do this fucking shit to me!" I yelled and fell to my knees.

◻ ◻ ◻

"Come sit down, bruh, you making me nervous," Loc called out.

"Nah, fuck that. They taking all day!" I spat. An officer walked up with a notepad.

"How you doing? Are you the family of the young lady that was in the accident, I have a few questions?"

"Yeah, what's up, is she okay?" I asked.

"I'm not sure I was trying to get some information about the accident. Do you know what happened?"

"Yeah, I was actually trailing her to her grandmother's house. We had just left the funeral home. When the light turned green, she started to go, and out of nowhere, I guess the other car ran the light and ran straight into her," I told him. He jotted some shit on his notepad.

"Are you aware that we found open containers of alcohol in her car?" He smirked.

"I don't give a fuck if a liquor store was in that bitch. That driver ran the fucking red light!" I yelled, and Loc grabbed me. I don't know if the officer got a thrill out of that shit because his smirk is what did it to me.

"Go do your job and harass the motherfuckers that ran the light," I barked.

"Family of Sherity Tyree!" the doctor entered the room.

"How is she doc?" I ran up to him.

"Everything is a bit touch and go right now, but we're trying to stop the bleeding. I just wanted to give you an update. She's about to head to surgery, so I will keep you updated," he informed us.

"Wait, did he just say Sherity Tyree? Lord, what done happened?" some girl hopped up and asked. I had never seen shorty in my life.

"Who is you?" I mugged the shit out of her.

"I'm Shameese. I just got off the phone with her about an hour ago telling her they rushed granny to the hospital she said she was on her way here," she started to cry. I ran my hands over my face and let out a huge sigh.

"She was in a horrible wreck and shit ain't looking too good," I hit the wall with my fist and Loc grabbed me to sit me down.

"This can't be I can't lose her too after I just found her again," Shameese cried. Loc was like a damn stretch Armstrong dog because he was trying to console both of us.

"What you mean too?" I asked, hoping she wasn't about to delivery more unpleasant news.

"Our granny just died," she cried.

"Man, I need a blunt," Loc blew out. All I did was hold my head down because this shit was just too much.

Two Months Later

Once the elevator stopped, I got off and walked past the desk of the nurses I had gotten familiar with over the last couple of months.

"Hey, Don!" one nurse spoke, who always seem to get extra friendly with a nigga. I hit her with a head nod and continued to Sherity's room.

When I walked in, I placed the fresh flowers that I had got in the vase and tossed the other ones in the trash. I adjusted the obituaries of Taylor and her granny that I had propped up against it. Walking over to the bed, I bent down and kissed SheShe on her lips.

After surgery, Sherity slipped in a coma where she stayed for a couple of weeks. Her brain wasn't responding well, and she ended up blacking out into another one. I don't know if my baby wasn't ready for the world or not, but she had a nigga on pins and needles. From what the doctors say, her body had healed from the initial trauma of the wreck, and they were running more tests to see what was going on.

"Hey baby, let this be the day you wake up because a nigga's tired of this hospital. I brought you some more flowers today," I told her.

The door of the room opened and in walked a spitting image of Sherity.

"Who are you?" I asked. The lady turned her nose up and waltzed her ass over to the bed.

"I'm Sherity's mother, and who are you?" she asked. I laughed when she had the nerve to say mother.

"Do I amuse you or something?" she asked.

"You amuse the fuck out of me. You're the same mother

that disowned her own child when she told you your sick ass son was raping her?" I spat. Her mouth dropped.

"You don't know shit about my son. It's clear she done fed you the same lies she been spewing for years."

"Oh, I know your bitch ass, son. Your son killed my sister, and I killed that sick ass motherfucker!" I spat with so much venom. I witnessed the way her eyes changed. She took my face in and then placed her hands over her chest.

"Why are you even out of jail, and what are you doing here with her?" she yelled.

"I did my time bitch, and this my fiancée. That's why I'm here," I replied and crossed my arms over my chest.

This lady looked like she was about to die on the spot. The door opened and in walked Shameese. When she saw Sherity's mother, she was just as shocked.

"What are you doing here, Auntie?" she asked.

"Oh great, the liars of the family have linked up. Why you ain't tell me my mama died?" she asked. This lady was crazy.

"It's funny that you cut granny off for believing Sherity and me now you pop up three months after she in the ground acting concerned. Don't worry. She left nothing to you." Shameese laughed.

"The only thing I want to know is why is it so hard to believe that your son did the things that he did to your daughter, niece, my sister, and plenty other girls? It's clear that nigga had a problem. You are a woman I can't just understand that," I had to ask.

"Rasheed was my firstborn and my baby. I taught him everything he knew and raised him right," she said with guilt in her eyes.

"It makes me wonder what exactly it was you taught him,"

Shameese said, and she lifted her brow at her auntie.

"Fuck you, you little bitch!" Sherity's mom spat.

"Nah, I think that's why we in this predicament now," Shameese shook her head, and I started to piece together little shit that she was saying but not really saying.

Sherity mom stormed out the room so fast, and I looked at Shameese.

"The fuck was that all about?" I whispered.

"Don, when I think back on things, more and more stands out. Her and Rasheed had a weird ass mother/ son bond. I think Rasheed was traumatized to the point he got obsessed with doing the same to as many girls as he could to hide his problem. I could be wrong, but I doubt it." She sighed.

"I thought I was fucked up," was all I could say.

Turning back around, I looked at my SheShe I knew whenever she woke up, I would get the best part of her. Come to find out it was a drunk driver that hit her, and they weren't even supposed to be driving due to past DUIs. Sherity fingers started to move, and I ran over to the bed.

"Did you see that?" I asked Shameese.

"Sherity, move your fingers again," I said excitedly. This time Sherity not only moved her fingers, but she opened her eyes. Shameese gasped and started pressing the nurse call button.

"Yes!" the nurse answered.

"She's up!" she yelled. Sherity tried to sit up.

"No baby hold on, you connected to some shit," I told her. I could tell she was frightened. The nurses came flying in the room, and I moved out of the way to let them do they job. Shameese and I both were looking on in anticipation. The doctor entered the room.

"I was just about to come and deliver some news," he said and walked over to Sherity. The nurse had a cup of water.

"I'm about to remove your tube out of your mouth. As soon as I do so, drink this," she instructed her. The nurse proceeded to remove the tube and then handed Sherity her water. To see Sherity drinking water had a nigga crying.

"So, what's up doc, is she good?" I asked.

"She is perfectly fine. It was like her body did a hard reset, but that isn't the news that I was coming to bear. After running a few more tests, it seems to me she was holding on because in about seven months, she has to be a mommy to this little one growing in there," he said, and I almost hit the floor.

"How the fuck that happened?" I barked.

"She had to literally just got pregnant before her accident, so the fact that it made it through the trauma is a blessing within itself. She's nine weeks along, and this I would say is a miracle baby." He smiled. Shameese was cheesing, and I looked at Sherity, who looked at me with puppy dog eyes. I walked over to the bed.

"Did you hear that?" I asked. Instead of speaking, she nodded her head.

"Does your throat hurt?" I asked, and she nodded her head again. She slowly opened her mouth and took another sip of water.

"They, they told me," she struggled to say.

"Who told you what?" I asked.

"Taylor and gran, granny a-a bout baby," she strained to get out. At this point, I didn't care who the fuck told her what. I had my girl back, and she was healthy and alcohol-free. I placed my hand on her stomach, and she slowly put hers on top of mine.

EPILOGUE
SHERITY

A Year Later

To have that feeling that your life is over is one that I never want to feel again. It was like I pleaded with God to give me another chance to get things right. While I was on my journey, that's what I call the place I went to while I was in a coma. I discovered a side to me that I didn't know I had. My granny and Taylor were there in my dreams and in my head the entire time. I vowed to never touch another drink again in an abusive tone. Occasionally I would have a glass of wine here and there, and that was it.

No one ever spoke on the things I overheard my mother say the day she came into my hospital room, and I pretended as if I didn't hear the conversation. My mother needed her own help, and I couldn't afford to let her bring any more pain into my life. I knew my brother was sick in the head, but a sick individual hurt him also. I'm not excusing the pain he caused others, and I still thank God for Don taking him up out of here.

When I gave birth to my daughter, it changed me. I felt I had to protect her like somebody should've done me. I was forever grateful for Don in so many ways. Who ever knew that a person so throwed off as him would be a gentle giant?

Placing the flowers on the grave, I looked at the rose gold headstone for Taylor, and I smiled.

"Happy Birthday, Taylor!" I sighed.

Taylor's death still affected me because we had so many wonderful times together that everything reminded me of him. I no longer heard his voice or saw him, so I took that as I was were, he was trying to get me, I had reached that point of not needing him anymore.

Turning around, I grabbed my five-month-old daughter out of her father's arms.

"Say bye, Tay'Lor," I cooed to a smiling Tay'Lor. Don and I named our daughter Tay'Lor Donnae Telhide after Taylor and, of course, his sister Donna.

"Mama said she would meet us at the house to get Tay'Lor, so we won't be late for our session," Don said as we walked back to the car. Don's mom had been the best granny ever. She said it was like having Donna all over again.

"I guess we better get going then." Don opened the backdoor, and I strapped the baby in her seat. When I climbed in the front seat, I looked over at my man. I was happy, mending, and loved with no complaints whatsoever.

DON

When I found out that Sherity was pregnant, I knew then that I was in this for the long haul. She remained in the hospital a few days after that, but once she was released, our real journey started. While I had opened a second moving company while she was in a coma, I had also opened one in Atlanta, putting me at three companies. Don't get me wrong. I was still that nigga, and Loc and I were still bringing in Win a right smart amount of money. I just moved a bit differently once I had a family to support.

The last time I saw my sister was when Tay'Lor was born because I just wasn't ready to let her go. The therapy sessions that both Sherity and I take was helping with our grievances as well. Folks might laugh and think that shit crazy that we're both in counseling and even family counseling, but we knew we needed help beyond what we could provide to fully heal from the things that damaged us.

When I told SheShe that I would protect her, I meant that in every aspect down to her heart, to her mental, to the bottoms of her soul, I was going to do what I had to do. She was my first love outside of my family, and hell, she was gone be my last. Now that we were actually together, I still had a hothead when it came to niggas looking at my girl and shit, but I was working on that.

I know that I've been calling her my fiancée, but I want us to be all the way together when we take that walk down the aisle for forever. We had a few more months left in the couple's part, and I didn't mind the work on myself as well as Sherity. I honestly would like for it to be ongoing. I know it takes longer than a year to heal from over twelve years of trauma, but I was riding. A nigga's got a soul now, and my heart belonged to SheShe and Tay'Lor.

I reached over and grabbed Sherity hand as I kept my eyes on the road. When our souls intertwined, you could physically feel that shit when we touched.

"I love you, SheShe." I glanced at her.

"Love don't love nobody," she had the nerve to say. When she saw my face changed, she stopped laughing.

"Who told you that shit?" I asked, knowing it was nobody but Loc's ass.

"Man, Loc's ass told me that the other day. I'm sorry, baby, you know I love you too," she smiled. I lifted her hand and kissed the back of it.

"You know a nigga no longer black-hearted," I winked.

THE END

FROM THE AUTHOR

Thank you for reading. Most importantly, thank you for continuing to support while on my independent journey. Please leave a review good or bad on Amazon or Goodreads.

KYEATE'S CATALOG

Games He Play: Di'mond & Kyng

A Savage and his Lady (Standalone)

Masking My Pain (Standalone)

Fiyah & Desire: Down to ride for a Boss (Standalone)

Securing the Bag and His Heart (Standalone)

Remnants (Novella)

5 Miles Until Empty (Novella)

Once Upon a Hood Love: A Nashville Fairytale (Novella)

Tricked: A Halloween Love Story (Novella)

Dear Saint Nik (Novella)

Kali Kusain: Counterfeit Queen (standalone)

My First Night with You: A BWWM Novella

Enticed by a Cold-Hearted Menace (Standalone)

Me vs. Me: Life of Deceit (Double book)

Her Mended Soul (Standalone)

Taking A Thug's Love (Standalone)

Valuable Pain: Money, Lies & Heartbreak (standalone)

Eboneigh: A Boss Christmas Tale (novella)

Unsteady Love From A Thug (Series)

Unsteady love from a thug 2

Tangled Lace (Standalone)

Another Lifetime (Novella)

From A Distance (Novella)

The Take: Rag$ to Riche$ (Standalone)

CPSIA information can be obtained
at www.ICGtesting.com
Printed in the USA
LVHW041734011020
667692LV00003B/509